CARTER BURST
INTO DOBRINI'S OFFICE

He was already at the desk when Dobrini reached into a side drawer. Carter kicked it shut on Dobrini's hand.

The howl of pain ended quickly when Carter's fist slammed the other's belly. Dobrini sailed across the room.

Carter picked Dobrini up by the front of his shirt and shook him. "We're going to talk," he said.

NICK CARTER IS IT!

"Nick Carter out-Bonds James Bond."
—*Buffalo Evening News*

"Nick Carter is America's #1 espionage agent."
—*Variety*

"Nick Carter is razor-sharp suspense."
—*King Features*

"Nick Carter has attracted an army of addicted readers . . . the books are fast, have plenty of action and just the right degree of sex . . . Nick Carter is the American James Bond, suave, sophisticated, a killer with both the ladies and the enemy."
—*The New York Times*

FROM THE NICK CARTER
KILLMASTER SERIES

SPYKILLER

KILL MASTER

NICK CARTER

JOVE BOOKS, NEW YORK

KILLMASTER #238: SPYKILLER

A Jove Book / published by arrangement with
The Condé Nast Publications, Inc.

PRINTING HISTORY
Jove edition / June 1988

ISBN: 0-515-09584-2

Jove Books are published by The Berkley Publishing Group,
200 Madison Avenue, New York, New York 10016.
The name "JOVE" and the "J" logo
are trademarks belonging to Jove Publications, Inc.

PRINTED IN THE UNITED STATES OF AMERICA

10 9 8 7 6 5 4 3 2 1

*Dedicated to the men of the
Secret Services of the
United States of America*

ONE

Felipe Zapato, his body all in black, was only a shadow in the grove of olive trees. Across the cypress-lined road, behind high wrought-iron gates and an equally high stone wall, loomed a huge, tile-roofed house. On a small plaque beside the gate, one word gleamed in brass script: BALARIA.

It was almost four in the morning. The last light in the huge villa had been extinguished an hour before. The sky above the wealthy resort area of Marbella in southern Spain was cloudy, obscuring the moon completely.

All was right.

It was time for Felipe Zapato to go to work.

He dropped from his perch in an olive tree and, like a cat, moved across the road. Every movement was precise, timed, as he uncoiled the rope from his shoulder. At the wall, the rope whistled upward and slipped silently over an iron spike. In seconds he was up the rope and moving along the wall. A leap of eight feet and he was in the first tree. Then, like a monkey, he was through the trees and directly beneath a balcony.

Again the rope whistled through the air, and the little thief hoisted himself up and over the balcony railing.

He had watched the villa of the Contessa Beatriz Balaria for nearly two weeks. All the windows on the first and second floors were securely locked at night, and on an alarm system. But the countess liked fresh air. She always slept with the doors to her third-floor balcony bedroom slightly open.

Zapato crouched, staring into the bedroom. At the side of a four-poster bed, a shaded light burned. A white silk coverlet obscured only the bottom half of a beautiful woman. She was nude and her bare breasts rose and fell evenly in the dim light.

Without making a sound, Zapato moved around the bed, pausing just long enough to tug the coverlet up to her chin: a cold person woke more readily than a warm one. This done, he tiptoed silently into the corridor and down the wide marble staircase.

The double doors to the first-floor study were locked. Now into the action, Zapato's stomach had lost its knot of fear and his gloved hands worked surely. Gentle fingers fitted the nose of a many-pronged master key into a pair of forceps. Exerting pressure with both hands, he turned the forceps against the lock until the tumblers clicked.

Completing the circle, he stood back, wetting his mouth. As always, sweat had started to drench the back of his shirt.

He rotated the door handle, pushing gently. The oak door stood ajar, and Zapato waited in the warm rush of air, heavy with a scent no longer fresh. Silently he prayed that the whore, Varga, had been correct with her information.

The velvet drapes were drawn. Zapato closed the door behind him and took a flash from his pocket. Quickly he played it over the walls, recalling Maria Varga's words: "My sister says the panel is between two paintings of the countryside, and the release catch is in the baseboard."

Zapato found the catch, and his heart pounded when the

panel slid aside to reveal the safe.

It was a Swiss Zorloch with a four-tumbler system. Not difficult for a man of Zapato's talents, but time-consuming.

From a belt around his middle he took two magnets, a stethoscope, and a tiny rubber mallet similar to those used by piano tuners.

The first tumbler fell into place and locked at once. It took him nearly a half hour for the other three. Once the safe was open, it took Zapato far less time to discover that the velvet boxes inside it contained only glass and paste.

"Daughter of a whore! Ignorant bitch!" he hissed, opening case after case, only to find more of the same.

He was about to throw them across the room in disgust, when the light held in his teeth fell across a barely discernible seam across the safe's inner lining.

Zapato recognized it at once: a safe within a safe. This one was a different brand and had a different kind of opening method: electrical impulses.

He searched the room thoroughly for some kind of send device, but he could find nothing. He was about to give up, when his eye fell on the television remote control. A quick investigation told him that the device had been altered.

The combinations of numbers could have been endless, but Zapato was a student of the human mind as well as a master thief.

He tried the license on the countess's Rolls-Royce. He ran her telephone number forward and backward. This went on for several minutes, as he tried to reproduce the numbered sequences she would most logically use.

Nothing.

Cautiously, he slipped from the room and back up the stairs. Her purse was in the bath adjoining the bedroom. Armed with every conceivable number that had anything to do with the countess, he returned to the study.

The number on her passport, backward, was the key. It opened a deep, pull-out drawer.

Again Zapato cursed.

A thick black book. A smaller blue book. A packet of official-looking papers.

That was all.

But the seal of the United States of America on the packet of papers caught Zapato's interest. He read, and got much more interested. He looked through the two books, and his hands began to shake.

Contessa Beatriz Balaria was an agent of the United States government, and what he held in his hands was worth far more than the jewels he had hoped to get.

But what to do?

Leave them, he decided; it might take a great deal of time to get a bid. In that time, if they were discovered missing, the countess might have time to water down their worth.

Zapato reopened the black book. From it he copied down a name, Joanna Dubshek, an address, a telephone number, a profile and a job description, as well as a list of what the woman had access to in her job.

This done, Felipe Zapato replaced everything exactly as he had found it and exited the villa the same way he had entered.

It was an amber-lit little bar called the Moonglow, in the old quarter of Seville near the cathedral. Inside, the atmosphere was heavy with the scent of perfume and cigars and strong Spanish cigarettes.

The place was run by an old harridan called Mother Moon. Being an enterprising woman, she also ran a small hotel in the upper rooms that rented by the hour.

There was a long, dark-wood bar, and there were small, dark-wood tables. Mother Moon's whores always sat at the tables, never at the bar. Strictly speaking, they were not quite Mother Moon's whores. They were discreet young women—some not so young—who, for the privilege of working out of the Moonglow, paid Mother Moon a nightly advance whether they scored or not.

Maria Varga was one of the not-so-young ones. She spotted Felipe Zapato the moment he entered, waited a few minutes until he settled at a table, and then sauntered over.

"Well?"

"Paste . . . paste and glass, you bitch."

"No, impossible!" the startled woman replied. "My sister told me—"

"I don't care what your sister told you," Zapato growled, "all the stones were phony."

"Shit." She started to rise, but Zapato grabbed her wrist and pulled her back into the chair.

"But the evening might not have been a total loss."

Maria Varga's darting black eyes stopped moving and centered on his. "How so?"

"I found some papers, some information your friend in Algeciras might pay a great deal to obtain."

Her olive complexion lightened a shade or two and her hands began to tremble. "No . . . I don't work for them anymore."

"But you have in the past, Maria. You have helped the Communists with blackmail, you have made films . . ."

"But no more. I am afraid of them!"

"Maria, listen to me. Give me the man's name and address. Call him and make an appointment for me. If you do, you may never have to work on your back again."

She got even more nervous, but as Zapato talked of the fortune he would make—and her share of it—her greed overcame her fear.

Eventually she rose and left the club. Twenty minutes

later she was back, slipping a piece of paper across the table.

"He will see you at nine tomorrow morning."

"*Sí,* Maria. You will not regret it."

The red carpet was faded, and the sign near the elevator advertised the same services in three languages:

DOMINGO BOLIVAR
IMPORTS AND EXPORTS
MEZZANINE FLOOR

An arrow pointed up the stairway to the mezzanine.

Zapato's nerves were strung tight as he walked up the stairs. But he did not hesitate. He had as much confidence in his powers of persuasion as he did in his ability as a thief.

He had no political leanings either way, and he had never worked with or for the Communists. But he knew that for what he had, they would be the best customer.

Zapato entered without knocking. Domingo Bolivar was reading the Paris edition of the *International Herald Tribune* in a cluttered cubbyhole that served as his office. He barely looked up when the door opened.

"Sorry . . . I thought there would be an outer office."

"I don't trust secretaries. You are Zapato?"

"*Sí.*"

"I am Domingo Bolivar. Shut the door and sit down."

Zapato did, not feeling quite as sure of himself as he had coming up the stairs. Bolivar took off his glasses and peered at him under the lampshade on the desk. His smile was oily.

"Since you come from Maria Varga, I assume you are a pimp."

"No. I am a thief."

"Ah, an honorable profession," Bolivar said, nodding, his oily smile growing wider. "What can I do for you?"

6

Zapato hesitated, eyeing Bolivar with growing unease. Bolivar was a heavy man, dressed in cotton trousers, a loose shirt, and slippers. Even though the morning was still cool, he oozed sweat.

"I have some information I am sure you would like to obtain."

"Such as?"

"There is a woman . . . rich, influential, Spanish. She has business connections in countries all over the world. She is also an agent of the American government."

Bolivar's dark eyes narrowed. "Who is this woman?"

Zapato smiled and ignored the question. "She has some kind of a master code book, and another, larger book. In the larger book are names of men and women located all over Europe. In reading the details, I think these people are spies for America. I think this woman runs some kind of spy network."

Domingo Bolivar's only visible reaction was a lifting of his heavy black eyebrows. But in his chest his heart had begun to beat like a triphammer. He knew there was a huge network controlled in Europe from Spain. Could this insignificant little thief have discovered the control?

"What makes you think, Señor Zapato, that I would have use for this information?"

"Because you are an agent of the Communists."

Suddenly the tension was thick in the room. The silence was oppressive. Bolivar opened a humidor on his desk with stubby fingers, withdrew a cigar, and took his time lighting it.

"Señor, that is a very dangerous accusation. Very dangerous indeed."

Zapato shrugged. "But true. I have told you that I am a thief. I will also tell you that I am wanted by the police."

The fat man leaned forward on his elbows, staring intently, a wreath of blue smoke floating around his head. "Let us suppose that I might have a client for the information you speak of . . . . What would you require in return?"

"A half million American, and your experts fixing this so I can take up residency in another country . . . say, somewhere in South America."

Here, Zapato took a passport from his pocket and flipped it across the desk. Bolivar looked briefly at the passport, then up at him again, still smiling.

"What do you want done to it?"

"Change the number and name, set my birthday back ten years, and alter the date on the entry stamp so it won't be more than three months old when I leave. I'll dye my hair, pad myself around the middle, and have a new photograph taken. The only pictures they have of me are newspaper prints, and those date back years. They won't have any reason to look twice at a middle-aged tourist. Once I am out of the country, I'm safe."

"You are not afraid of extradition?"

"I don't think they will bother. I'm not that important."

The fat man leaned back and puffed heavily on the cigar. "The passport, of course, poses no problem. A half million, however, is a great deal of money, even for—"

"I have a sample." Zapato took the notebook from his pocket, tore out a page, and handed it to the other man. "I think the woman is a Pole or a Hungarian working in the Russian embassy in Rome."

Bolivar studied the slip of paper, and for the first time since Zapato had entered the office the smile faded from his lips.

"This will take some time, perhaps weeks, to check out. You said you were wanted. Do you have a safe house?"

"I do. I rent a small villa near Estepona under another name. I have an old woman who cooks and cleans for me.

She lives in a separate apartment. I rarely go out in the area, and most of my work was done previously in the north, around Madrid."

"And your only connection with me is this Maria Varga?"

Zapato nodded.

"I think it would be best that no one know about this meeting. Do you have any objections?"

Zapato shrugged. "None."

"I will be in touch. Good day, Señor Zapato."

Domingo Bolivar waited until the thief's footsteps had faded before he picked up the phone and dialed a number in Madrid.

"Hello?"

"Tony, I have work. I think you will enjoy it . . . a woman."

"When?"

"Can you still make the afternoon flight to Seville?"

"Yes, I'm sure of it."

"Good. And when that is done, I might be sending you back home for a few days."

"Rome?"

"Yes . . . another woman."

The rotund man hung up the phone and checked his watch. It was nearly eleven, time to vacate the office.

Quickly, he gathered up his papers from the desk and placed them in a briefcase. This done, he checked the office to make sure everything was as he had left it, and moved to the door. Just above the door ne flipped a small button that would kill the relay phone.

Then he moved into the hall and locked the door behind him. He huffed his huge bulk up one flight and opened another door, this one marked ALEXANDER CZARKIS, ACCOUNTANT.

TWO

Rome, Tony Lucchi thought; that would be nice. He had grown to love Spain, and the work was constant, but it would be nice to visit his homeland again, even for a short visit.

But first there was Seville.

He showered and shaved. In the bedroom, he dressed in a white shirt and a conservative tie and a nondescript suit. He put money in his wallet, plenty of money, and an alternate set of identification.

He looked in the mirror and grinned. He had big, fine white teeth. He had a pleasant, engagingly boyish grin. He was extremely handsome and he knew it. It was his looks and charm that often gave him the extra edge in his work.

One more look in the mirror, and he left the apartment. Halfway to the elevator, he remembered and returned. He rummaged through a small, hidden drawer in the rear of a dresser until he found it: long and slim and graceful, a six-inch switchblade.

He placed it and some underclothes in a small overnight bag, then went out into the warm night to hail a cab.

Tony Lucchi, tall and handsome and loaded with money.

11

A combination few women could resist.

In Seville, Tony Lucchi bought a newspaper, a city map, and rented a car. Using the map and the newspaper, it took him an hour to find what he wanted, a small house in a secluded, not heavily populated area. The house was for lease, fully furnished, and had a private garage with a door directly into the kitchen.

He killed time until dark, then found a store where he purchased several bottles of liquor and wine.

The neighborhood was quiet when he returned to the house. It took ten seconds to jimmy the lock on the garage. Seconds after that, he had the car and the To Let sign in the garage. He carried his packages into the house and, after closing all the drapes, snapped on a few very dim lights. When he had managed to give the house a rumpled, lived-in look, he returned to the garage and headed for the Moonglow.

The bar was crowded with men. None of them gave Lucchi a second look. Not so with the women. They all looked, and liked what they saw. They all bedded down for money, but it was a lot easier if the bed partner looked like Tony Lucchi.

He didn't see a woman who fit the description he had of Maria Varga. Most of them were either older or younger, shorter or fatter. Nevertheless, he chatted up three of the women just in case.

Then he saw her enter: tall, good figure, long, glossy black hair, a worn, tired face. He even heard one of the other girls call out to her by name.

She took a corner table and Lucchi made his move before anyone else could get to her.

"May I?" he said.

She looked up with narrow dark eyes that, for the briefest of seconds, were fearful. Then they took in his boyish good looks and softened. "Beg pardon?"

"May I . . . buy you a drink?"

A little grin began at the corner of her mouth. "Are you sure . . . ?"

"I'm sure."

She nodded and Lucchi sat. It was a little table. His knees touched hers, and hers touched back.

The waiter came.

"Wine," she said.

"Wine," he echoed.

The waiter moved away, and Maria leaned forward. Her grin was full now. "You are quick, aren't you?"

"Me?" he asked innocently.

"I hardly just came in."

"You're very pretty."

She was not pretty. She had a long nose and thin lips and a sallow complexion, and she was at least thirty-five, maybe more. But her teeth were good, and her affable smile made dimples in her cheeks, and her bare arms were smooth and firm. Inside that short black skirt was a crazy, wonderful figure; on top she was wearing a flimsy, see-through blouse trimmed strategically with lace. "Very pretty indeed," he said.

"Don't kid an old lady."

"But you are," he insisted.

"In the eye of the beholder," she said.

"And you've got a wild figure."

"That, yes. That, in all modesty, I have to admit. Once upon a time I was a dancer. But my hips got too damn big."

"Not at all."

"Look, any woman, if she knows how, can hang on to her figure. I would say my figure's just the same as when I was a girl. But the backside—excuse the expression—that, you can't do much about. When it starts bulging out on you, it's like, well, a despair."

The waiter brought the wine and Tony Lucchi paid.

"What's your name?"

"Anthony. You?"

"Maria. You're not Spanish."

"American, but I live here, in Seville."

She lit a cigarette. "You've never been here before."

"No."

"I'm not like the other girls," she said, dragging deeply and sipping the wine.

"Oh?" Lucchi said, glancing around.

"I only go out with a man who excites me."

"Do I excite you?"

"Maybe," she said, and smiled. "Are you liberal?"

It was Lucchi's turn to smile. "I don't suppose you mean my politics."

"No." Now the heavily mascaraed dark eyes appraised him carefully. The suit was plain but expensive, the tie was expensive, the shirt was expensive. He was too pretty for the neighborhood, but he wasn't police. Police didn't dress like that. They couldn't afford it. "Tony, you want to party?"

"I want to party," he said, adding, "all night."

"That's expensive."

"How expensive?"

"Twelve," she replied with a straight face.

Lucchi suppressed a grin. Twelve thousand pesetas, nearly a hundred dollars. She had never made that in her life.

"I think we've got a party," he said. "My place? My wife's out of town."

"Fine," she said with a shrug.

"And would you mind if we left separately? My wife . . . it's a green, two-door Torino. I'll watch for you."

"You're paying," Maria said, shrugging again.

He dropped a tip on the table and left. She waited five minutes, then left herself, pausing at a pay phone in the foyer.

"Carla, it's me. Has that bastard Felipe called?"

"No, Maria," her sister replied in a slurred voice, "nobody calls."

"Carla, for God's sake, you're drunk. I told you—"

"I'm sorry, I couldn't help it. I'm sorry."

"Yes, I know. Go to bed, Carla. I'll be out all night."

Maria hung up and walked out into the street. The Torino was about a half block away. He was smiling at her through the open door.

God, he was handsome, and young. Just what she needed tonight.

She got in and snuggled close to him. "You may not believe this, Anthony, but you're going to be good for me tonight."

Tony Lucchi was smiling broadly as he pulled away from the curb.

"Sí, sí," he said. "Very good for you."

"Nice house."

"Glad you like it. Get comfortable. Wine?"

"Sí, wine," she said, "lots of it."

She found the radio and turned the dial. Soft flamenco guitar music filled the room. He poured and handed her a glass. She swayed as she drank, dancing to the music.

"I think I'm a little drunk," she giggled.

He took her in his arms and danced with her. As she molded against him with a sigh, he kissed her, his tongue in her mouth.

When she could talk she said, "Know something?"

"What?"

"I don't kiss. I mean on the mouth. I don't kiss customers."

"You kissed me."

"I don't feel you're like a customer. But business is business. Know what I mean?"

He broke from her, and she danced alone.

He took money from his wallet and gave it to her.

"I'll treat it like a gift."

He took out more and gave it to her.

"Why?" she said, and danced around him, waving the money.

"Let's just say you're a good investment."

Had Maria Varga been more alert, she would have noticed the new, flat tone that had crept into his voice. As it was, she only danced to her purse and deposited the money.

Lucchi watched her and removed his clothes, then he took her in his arms and danced her into the bedroom. The overnight bag was open, by the bed.

Her left arm was around him. Her right hand moved between them and found him. "Hmmm, all man," she purred. "A warrior!"

"I told you I'd kill you."

"Like that I'm willing to die," she sighed.

"Get naked," he said.

"I'm going to do that."

"Do it," he said.

"Like slow?"

"Like any way you want," he said.

"Like a striptease?" She smiled coyly.

"Just do it."

To the rhythm of the music, she opened her blouse and flung it off. To the rhythm of the music, she unzipped her skirt, let it drop, and kicked it away. And kicked out of her shoes. No stockings. A pink bra and pink panties around the big, broad, round, marvelous body, and the musky odor of her encompassed him.

"Nice," he said.

She unhooked the bra and, still dancing, tossed it to him. He tossed it away as she wriggled out of the panties. Then she was dancing wildly, arms upraised, breasts bobbing, stomach heaving, pubis churning.

"Come here."

She did, and he flipped her to the side. She landed on the bed on her back, her legs high and wide, and he was over her.

He grabbed and seized. He kissed up over her belly, her breasts, then entered her savagely.

"Oh yes . . . my God . . . oh, my God!"

Her legs scissored around him and she thrashed beneath him, no longer a whore but a woman caught in the throes of rampant desire.

Above her, he became a machine. Her eyes were closed, so she didn't see the way his eyes glazed as he pummeled. She babbled, urging him to continue, to never stop.

And he didn't stop. On and on, turning her, twisting her in positions she had never been in before. God, he was wild, a lunatic, a lunatic lover.

He had her at the top of the mountain and wouldn't let her come down.

God, I should pay him!

She opened her eyes and looked up at him. He was out of this world.

My God, she thought, *look at his eyes* . . . . Black, shiny, crazy black, shiny eyes. And the face . . . innocent, youthful, no lines, no cares, a boy's face. Only the eyes gave him away, told her what a madman he was.

Maria Varga closed her eyes again and a flood of release swept over her.

She never noticed the odd way he stretched over the side of the bed. She didn't hear the faint click as the razor-sharp blade snapped out of the hilt.

She screamed once, and then felt nothing.

THREE

The villa was small, just off Via della Lungara, overlooking the Tiber. It had only been in use for about six months. That was the usual routine for AXE safe houses; short-term leases, then moving to another area. When its current inhabitant left, it would probably be closed down, the keys handed back to the estate agent, and another house set up within a week.

The current resident had been in place for three days. His name was Carter, Nick Carter, top gun for supersecret AXE. Right now, Carter, dressed to the nines in a white dinner jacket, dark razor-creased trousers, and black patent leather shoes, paced the second-floor study of the villa.

Two hours earlier he had made the contact, playing a well-dressed security guard at the American embassy. It was one of those affairs where dinner was served to about thirty guests assembled from all the embassies in Rome. They were supposed to sit around, eat, talk, and make believe that just over the horizon there would be mutual understanding.

Five days earlier, Carter had been in Nice, France, taking the sun and a well-deserved rest. Word had come from AXE

19

chief of operations in Washington, David Hawk.

"Balaria has a pickup in Rome . . . could be a delicate situation . . . blackmail. Assess and handle."

The agents in Beatriz Balaria's black book were top-notch people. When they wanted a pickup, the information was usually hot and needed immediate attention. The job often fell to an AXE operative.

In this case, the provider was an intelligence research analyst in the Russian embassy, a woman of Polish descent named Joanna Dubshek.

The contact was made through notes passed by two waiters, and the meeting was set.

Her needs were odd: a screen and a Russian-type ALM 8mm projector with sound capabilities. Carter had been forced to hustle, but the proper equipment had been found and was now set up.

But where was Joanna Dubshek?

At the window he sipped his scotch and peered through the night at the winding road that led down to the big boulevard and the Tiber beyond.

He pictured Joanna Dubshek in the brief moment he had seen her earlier, cocktail in hand, at the dinner party. She was young, much younger than Carter had expected, and the figure-hugging green satiny dress she had been wearing didn't give her age.

Moving through the crowd, chatting like the good little information-gathering machine she was supposed to be for the Soviet Union at these affairs, she had looked more like a Hollywood starlet than a spy.

Her skin glowed with a tawny hue, as if her veins were full of honey. She was tall and lithe with high, full breasts and long, supple legs. A veil of silver-gold hair streaked lightly by the Italian sun framed a remarkable face. Unlike most Poles it was narrow, with high cheekbones and a petite mouth. Even her nose was delicate, patrician, with an insouciant tilt.

It was a pity, Carter thought, that they would only be together for a short time.

But business was business. Maybe, when this was over, he could sneak back up to Nice for a few more days.

Then he saw the lights, yellow, on dim. She was being cautious. Just off the main boulevard they went out completely. Carter saw her park two blocks away. He measured the time and opened the door the moment she knocked.

"Come in."

She moved quickly by him and Carter closed the door. She was carrying a small canvas airline bag. She had changed from the green gown into a dark blue, short-skirted suit, pinched in at the waist. It accented her already incendiary figure, and Carter silently moaned that the night would be all business.

"Something to drink?"

"I could use a brandy."

Carter talked while he poured. "Any trouble?"

"I don't think so. I returned to the compound after the party, changed, and left by the servants' gate. I have a car parked by the Palazzo Barberini for nights like this. It's leased under another name. They don't know about it. I took two cabs to the car and drove here a very roundabout way."

He brought her a snifter. She set down the valise and took the brandy gratefully.

"What have we got?" Carter asked.

Joanna sipped, set the glass aside, and crossed the room to the equipment. She glanced at the set-up screen, moved to the projector, examined it, and nodded.

"Can you handle this?"

"In a pinch," Carter replied.

"No matter, I can. Did you set up the transfer lab?"

He nodded. "Ready to go at a moment's notice."

"Good," she said, bending to the bag. "This has to be back in the vault by morning."

She extracted a small can of film from the bag and removed the film from the can. Quite expertly, she threaded the film into the projector.

"Would you please dim the lights?"

Carter moved to kill all the lights except a small lamp.

"There are five full rolls. I think you'll only need to see one. I'm sure you'll want to have all five transferred to video tape."

"Okay, roll it," Carter said, settling back in the sofa.

Joanna hit a button on the projector and the screen came fuzzily alive. A few adjustments and the picture cleared.

Carter saw a beautiful living room, the color scheme a subtle blend of gold, green, and rose. A door opened and a tall, dark-haired woman entered.

Right behind her came a stocky man in an expensively tailored sports coat. He had the rough-and-ready look of a mechanic, strongly built, firm-jawed, steady, with energetic eyes. Between the gray hair and the seamed face, Carter guessed him to be in his late fifties.

"The man is Sydney Lockwood. When this film was taken, about a year ago, he was in Seville as head of a new radar project for MacPherson Aviation. He was there for two months to test the system."

"The apartment?"

"Rented by a local businessman, paid for by the KGB. It's used almost exclusively for what you're seeing."

What Carter was seeing was Sydney Lockwood kissing and pawing the woman. Eventually the woman managed to come up for air.

"Isn't this nice? Didn't I tell you it would be?" she gasped.

22

"And my boyfriend is away on vacation. Better than a hotel!"

"Yeah, yeah," Lockwood growled, and went after her again.

It wasn't long before he had ripped off his clothes and started working on the woman's. She was well over thirty and far from beautiful, but she had a mouth-watering figure.

"Who's the woman?"

"We don't know," Joanna replied. "She has been used quite often by the control in the area, one Domingo Bolivar."

The couple was on the floor by now, Lockwood in the saddle and riding for home. The look on his face made Carter feel that the man was on the way to heaven.

The woman's expression was bland and somewhat impatient, the pained but sympathetic look of a schoolteacher reciting poetry by rote to a roomful of bored teen-agers.

Lockwood got the job done and rolled away. The woman fixed drinks and they smoked and talked.

Three minutes into the conversation, it got interesting. Ten minutes later, Carter was on the edge of his chair.

"Jesus Christ, he's reciting the findings of all the radar tests since he's been there!"

"I thought that would interest you," Joanna Dubshek said. "As you can see, she's hardly paying attention. I figure he's just talking shop to himself, thinking she wouldn't understand a word of it, and doesn't have the brains to remember much of it anyway."

Carter agreed. "She's no trained swallow. Probably a local hooker."

"I guess the same. Lockwood wouldn't talk like that to a pro. He would spot her."

After fifteen minutes of blatant breaches of security, Sydney Lockwood was ready again.

This time the woman took over with a lascivious smile on her face. It was fairly obvious that she could tear the man up if she were in the mood. This second time around, she was definitely in the mood.

"Does it go on like this?" Carter asked.

"Clear to the end of the film. Mr. Lockwood is a vigorous man."

"Shut it off."

Joanna did, and Carter upped the lights before freshening their drinks.

"The other four films . . . are they the same?"

"Substantially, only more so. A second woman, younger, prettier, makes up a kinky threesome on two of them. On all of them, Lockwood talks a lot."

"You say these were taken about a year ago?"

Joanna nodded. "Over a period of two months. Until now they were used only for the information on the tapes. That's changed. We're to make copies and get them to a KGB control in Washington. Blackmail."

"Why now?"

"Because Sydney Lockwood has been made head of procurement for MacPherson Aviation."

Carter whistled. MacPherson had their hands in over half of the Pentagon pie. As head of procurement, every plan for bids would go through Lockwood's hands, as well as every nut and bolt if a bid were accepted. He would also know the status of progress on every project.

"Other than the obvious, what else would make Lockwood knuckle under?"

"Old family, money, his father was a general, and he's happily married with three children."

"Jesus," Carter growled, "and he can't keep his pants on or his mouth shut."

"He's a typical man," Joanna Dubshek replied, and shifted to light a cigarette.

The shift lifted her skirt three-quarters of the way up a

beautifully curved thigh. Carter looked, thought about the film, shivered, and turned away to the bar.

"Rewind that one and put it back in the can." He poured and heard her working away behind him. "Got anything else, not on the tape?"

"Lots," she replied. "Memorized memos, routing orders to Washington, a little on this Domingo Bolivar, and some odds and ends."

Carter put the solo tape in the bag with the other four and took her by the hand. He opened the bedroom door, flipped on the light, and tugged her through.

"What are you . . ."

Before she finished the question, he had pulled her past the unmade bed and seated her at a small desk. On top of the desk was an uncovered typewriter.

"Put it all down, everything. I'll run the films to the lab and have them transferred to video cassettes."

Joanna checked her watch. "Can you be back in less than three hours? It's tricky if I don't slip back into the compound before dawn."

"I'll make sure."

Carter left her at the typewriter. He climbed into a shoulder rig and tucked his 9mm Luger, Wilhelmina, into the holster under his left armpit. He adjusted the spring sheath of his stiletto, Hugo, under his right sleeve, and pulled on a jacket.

The night was dark and quiet as he backed a small red Fiat out of the garage and rolled down the hill. At the gates he dropped the clutch and the engine came to life. He hit the Via della Lungara moving and turned left. A mile on, he turned right over the Tiber and then left again. He kept to the major streets to make time and drove like a maniac.

No one paid any attention. Everyone in Rome drove like a maniac.

He crossed the open expanse of Saint Peter's Square and

turned east into Trastevere, the ancient, densely populated section of Rome where streets twist and turn in every direction.

Twice he thought he spotted the same car and driver behind him, but couldn't be sure. Just in case, he cut north, then south, then north again, crisscrossing streets and turning haphazardly.

Satisfied, he found the tiny Via Colona and parked. A half block farther on, he turned through a gate into a small courtyard. There were three shops. Carter went to the center door and rang the bell. A tiny sign under the bell said EDUARDO PARMO, VIDEO TRADUZIONE.

The door was opened by a slender man in his late twenties, with dark blond hair and features that were just too delicate for a male face.

"You're early," Parmo said.

"I didn't have to take much time looking," Carter said, moving past him through the main area of the shop and into the rear equipment room. "Are you set up?"

"Of course," Parmo replied, walking around Carter and perching on a high stool in front of his equipment. "How many?"

"Five," Carter said, handing him the bag. "How long?"

"Two hours?" he asked, already threading one of the films. It flickered on a nearby monitor. "Oh, God, how gross!"

"To each his own sin," Carter growled. "Can you make it an hour and a half?"

"For you, of course."

"Thanks," Carter said dryly. "Anyplace close by where I can get a drink? I saw a bar on the corner."

"That would be Allesandro's. Don't go there."

"Why not?"

"Because that's where I go. The other way, middle of

the block. Turn into the alley, you'll see the sign, Taverna
Nello. More your style."

Carter hit the street, turned right, found the alley then
the sign. On the other side of the door was a hostess. She
was a tall, red-haired Dolly Parton in not enough green se-
quins to cover it all.

Parmo had been right.

The Taverna Nello was more his style.

Tony Lucchi slid from the roof on the thin, black nylon
line and dropped soundlessly to the deck of the balcony.
The line barely made a whisper as it slipped around the
chimney, off the roof, and into his hands. He coiled it and
checked the door.

It slid open without a sound, and Lucchi slipped into the
room. To his left he heard the steady pecking of a typewriter,
and moved toward it.

The bedroom door was ajar. She was seated, intent at the
typewriter, her profile to him. Her blond hair was pulled
back and pinned. She had small ears. Her feet under the
desk were shoeless. Her face, beautiful, gleamed with a
thin sheen of perspiration.

It was hot in the villa.

Beside her chair lay a suit jacket and a thin white blouse.
Obviously she had discarded them because of the heat, and
now she sat, typing, in her bra. She was big, the soft flesh
of her breasts filling the bra and bulging up over the cups
to tantalize him.

He had been watching her every move, even observed her
in her own bed, sleeping, for two weeks, and never had she
looked so beautiful and appealing.

Trembling, Lucchi backed off to ram the door.

"However you do it, Tony," Bolivar had said, "make sure
that we are not suspected. Make them think it was a thief,

a rapist, or even the Americans . . . anyone but us. That is important."

Dobrini and his brothers would take care of the big black-haired American. They would put him away for hours. There would be time.

Tony Lucchi carefully removed all his clothing as the typing continued. When he was completely naked, he strapped the sheath containing the switchblade to his right calf and moved back to the open bedroom door.

He was convinced he could take her without any trouble. He had read her file. She was in computers, trained only for that. She was big, inches taller than he, but he was an athlete, trained, a killer.

On silent feet he moved into the room behind her. Rapt in work, she gave him no heed. Rapt in work, she didn't sense his presence until she felt the cold steel of the knife at her throat.

"Get up slowly . . . turn around."

She did. "Who are you? What do you want?"

"Take off your clothes."

This can't be happening, Joanna thought. With all she had been through, with all the risks she had taken, she was about to be raped in an American safe house?

"Look . . ."

"Take off your clothes!"

She saw his eyes . . . shiny, black, cruel, wild. She felt the knife. She sensed his involuntary twitchings, saw the uncontrollable contractions in his small but well-muscled arms.

His face was that of a boy. His eyes were those of a maniac.

Then she began to remove her clothes.

Tony Lucchi's eyes followed every move.

God, he thought, she was beautiful. Tall, curved, skin

glistening, proud breasts rising and falling as she breathed fear.

"I have money in my purse."

He couldn't resist the impulse to laugh. "Money? Money is nothing compared to your body. Get on the bed!"

She hesitated.

He knew how to convince her. The knife was a blur as it shot forward and retreated. A thin line of red appeared on her arm from her shoulder to her elbow.

Joanna jumped. She was really frightened now. She had led a dangerous life, but until now she had never been in a life-threatening situation.

And this was life-threatening, obvious from the way he handled the lethal blade and the lunatic lust in his glazed eyes.

Give it to him. Get it over with. Perhaps Carter would return early . . .

"The bed," he said, his voice rising.

She made no further resistance. She lay on the bed, on her back, supine, quiet.

"Smart," he hissed, his lips splitting in a lewd grin. "I'm going to tie you, but loose, so you can have room to move."

He removed cords from the venetian blinds and tied her tight but loose. The knots were tight but there was sufficient play so she could move. He tied her wrists to either corner of the top of the bed, and her ankles to either corner of the bottom of the bed, and only then did he fully relinquish the knife. He laid it on the bedside table.

"See?" he said. "Did I hurt you? I didn't hurt you."

"Get it over with, bastard," Joanna spat.

The knife was inches from her head. She could almost touch it with her fingertips. The knots were loose.

The question was, were they loose enough?

He flung himself on her and kissed her, forcing her mouth

open by the pressure of his teeth on her lips. Revulsion filled Joanna, making her gag slightly, but she was able to move, to stretch her left arm.

The whole of his concentration was on her body now. He moved down. He gripped her breasts in his powerful hands, hurting her. His lips found her nipples and her body strained away from him, toward the knife.

And then he was on her, over her, and she had the knife. She flipped it around and began sawing.

She could feel the blade cut deeply into her wrist as she missed the rope and tried again. She could feel the blood spurting from her wrist, and the pain. But it was nothing compared to the pain of his sudden penetration.

She screamed.

Just as her wrist came free, he rose up, a leer on his lips, his shiny black eyes glazed, the pupils dancing as if the rape were like dope, making him high.

She struck in an arching slash. The blade ripped across his cheek, opening it from his ear to his mouth.

But before she could come back across his throat, he had her wrist in both his powerful hands.

It was futile.

He was growling like a wounded animal.

The blade was turning, being propelled downward toward her throat by his weight.

She felt nothing as the world went dark.

FOUR

It had been an hour, on the nose. Carter had consumed three of the watered whiskies. In between, he had rung up AXE Central in Rome, and gotten through to Joe Crifasi at once.

"Guiseppe, Carter."

"What's up?"

"It looks like a blackmail scam. Put a rush through to Washington. Have them put a surveillance team on one Sydney Lockwood. He's procurement and Pentagon liaison for MacPherson Aviation."

"He's the pigeon?"

"Right, and they've got enough to nail him to the cross. Parmo is copying five films on him now. Also, get me what you can on a Spaniard named Domingo Bolivar."

"What's his locale?"

"I'll know in a hour or so. Joanna Dubshek is typing me up a report with details right now."

"Check. Stay in touch."

"Will do."

Carter hung up and returned to the bar. He dropped some bills and headed for the door. Dolly watched him come with a smile.

"Must you leave so early?"

"Business."

She did a little shrug, and the earth shook. "We all have to work. I get off at four."

"In the morning?"

"I come from Spain," she said and grinned.

Carter slipped her a bill. "I'll be back."

In the alley, he lit a cigarette and checked his watch again by the glare of his lighter.

Eduardo Parmo should be just finishing. He headed for the dim light on Via Colona.

They jumped him just at the mouth of the alley, where it was still in darkness. Two of them at first, one from his right, another from his left. They came over the walls, and before he could go for the Luger, each of them had an arm.

A third, half the size of the other two, came up from behind a pile of garbage cans like a midget dynamo. He was in front of the Killmaster a split second after the other two had his arms, and the little man was swinging.

He landed a four-punch combination in the middle of Carter's gut so fast that his hands were only a blur. The Killmaster had no time to tense his stomach muscles, and before he knew it, he was gasping for air.

They were pros. All three of them knew exactly what they were doing and how to go about it.

When the little man moved his fists up to Carter's face and throat, the two monsters at his sides bent his arms nearly double and used their fists on his kidneys.

The Killmaster's body was used to punishment. At the training ground in Virginia, he was known as the Iron Man because of the mental and physical punishment he could absorb.

But not even iron could withstand for long the bruising blows these three were dishing out.

"Gun . . . shoulder rig," one of them barked in Italian.

"Get it!" answered the little man, and went back to Carter's gut.

He felt Wilhelmina's weight leave him and then he was slammed, face first, up against one of the brick walls and held there by the monsters.

Now the little boxer was at his kidneys, each punch driving his pelvis into the hard bricks.

The little guy was bound to get tired eventually, Carter hoped.

He did, taking a five-second, panting break.

Carter gathered up what strength he had left. Using the two big ones as a fulcrum, he kicked backward and connected. It was solid. He heard a grunt of surprise from the little man, and then a crash as he collided with the garbage cans.

Still in the air, Carter twisted and smashed his head into the one on his right. But he was a beat too late turning back to his left when he came down.

A freight train hit him in the jaw. A freight train of knuckles. His legs buckled under him, and he flew back. He couldn't stop moving. What was wrong? He tried to clear his head. He lifted his face, and his eyes began to focus. It was . . . .

The wall smashed into the back of his head. He felt himself falling, falling down onto the cobblestones.

His breath shot out of him as a foot smashed his ribs. He couldn't breathe. The air was like tongues of flame. Suddenly he felt blows everywhere. Sensations of pain rang out over his body, like sharp bells ringing too close.

In the midst of this, Carter heard his own voice, "Attack . . . fight, man, fight!"

Suddenly he could see. His mind was cleared. He was on his back and . . .

A foot was flying at him, a big black boot. He grabbed the foot and twisted it hard, throwing the person attached to it over him. Then he quickly rolled to the side and jumped to his feet.

All three of them were up again and circling silently around him. Carter flexed the muscle of his right forearm, his hand itching for the stiletto's hilt.

It never came. The spring-sheath had gotten twisted on his arm. It released the blade, but the knife became tangled in his cuff. Before he could free it, they were on him again.

Carter caught the punch in midair. He slipped under the man's arm and lifted a knee into his gut. He spun his whole body into it so that the knee whipped up, around, and smashed into the big stomach like a hammer.

The man's mouth flew open as the air shot out of him like a popped balloon. He fell, clutching his middle.

Carter heard something coming at him from behind. He leaped to the side. An eight-inch blackjack missed his head by inches.

The Killmaster jumped back before the second giant could aim his headcrusher once again. Quick as a cat, Carter slammed his elbow into the big man's face directly below the nose.

Something in the face cracked, and blood shot everywhere. The man growled in fury and went down, his hands over his mouth as if he had just eaten something raw he shouldn't have.

Carter whirled, still dizzy, his own blood flowing into his eyes.

The third one, the little one. Where the hell was he?

He heard the scrape but didn't get ready in time. He saw the two boots coming off the top of the wall directly at him.

His hands came up.

Too late.

The boots hit him, full force, center chest. He went back and down.

He felt, rather than heard, the back of his head hit the cobblestones.

And then he felt nothing.

He came to slowly, his face against something soft, a pillow, no, two pillows.

He opened his eyes. They hurt but he could see.

"Hello, Dolly."

"Dolly? I am Carmella. You are hurt. I will call an ambulance."

"No," he croaked. "Just a little argument between old friends."

He tried to rise, couldn't, and she hoisted him to his feet like a feather.

"You are hurt."

"Hurting," he replied with a groan, and checked. Sore, very sore, and bloody. But other than maybe a cracked rib or two, a split lip and busted hand, he was mobile.

"Come inside. I will clean you up."

He patted her cheek. "Any other time I'd take you up on that."

"One of them dropped this."

It was his Luger. The magazine had been ejected. "No, they didn't," he said, and slipped it into his shoulder rig.

"Come," she said.

"Rain check," he replied.

Leaving her shaking her head, he staggered to the street and, holding his sides, made it back to Eduardo Parmo's shop.

"Eduardo . . . Eduardo . . ."

Carter heard a groan and stumbled through the connecting door. Parmo was on the floor, moving like a crab. His left arm was useless and the back of his head was a mess.

Carter grabbed him and gently lowered him to his side. Tenderly, he applied fingertips to pressure points to stem the bleeding. It looked useless.

Parmo coughed. His eyes were closed, but his lips were moving, trying to make words.

"Nick . . ."

"Take it easy, Eduardo. I'll get help . . ."

"Nick, got three of them run off . . ."

"Yeah?"

Parmo coughed again and bloody foam spilled over his lips. "They got the films, all five . . . and two of the cassettes . . . but, Nick . . ."

He stopped. His head flopped to one side and his lips worked but no sound came out. Carter got his ear down, close to the man's mouth.

"Third tape . . . still in the machine . . . hit the rewind . . ."

His voice was so faint Carter could barely hear it.

"Rewind . . . Nick . . . cassette will load automatically . . . eject . . . Nick . . ."

No sound. He didn't move. His lips had gone slack.

Carter laid the lifeless, crushed head gently on the floor and walked to the machine. He hit the rewind button and the thing came to life.

While he waited, he lit a cigarette and unfuzzed his brain.

He remembered feeling guns in shoulder rigs on both of the big men. Besides the blackjacks, they probably also had knives. A crew like that would come prepared.

But they hadn't used anything but the blackjacks. Either they hadn't wanted to kill, or they wanted to make it look like a robbery.

Why?

And then it hit him. Time. They were buying time.

The cassette ejected. Carter grabbed and pocketed it and ran for the door. He sprinted down the street to his car.

The Killmaster knew it would take him close to twenty minutes to reach the villa. He started the Fiat's engine and yanked the wheel around in a U-turn. He thought about calling Crifasi, but there wasn't time now.

He made it in seventeen minutes, leaving a lot of cussing cabdrivers in his wake.

Veering the Fiat off the lane, he parked in the driveway under a tree. Joanna Dubshek's car was still where she had parked it.

His stomach turned into an aching knot when he hit the front door. It was ajar and one of the glass panels had been kicked out in the series of windows beside it.

Wilhelmina was empty. He palmed the stiletto and moved toward the bedroom. Carefully, he eased open the door.

Carter had seen death many times in many forms all over the world. He never remembered gagging.

Now he gagged and retched all the way back through the living room to the phone.

"Crifasi, Carter. I need you."

"Now?"

"Right now. I'm at the house. And bring a laundry crew . . . and a doctor. And send a pair to Parmo's. They'll need a body bag there as well."

"Oh, shit."

"My sentiments exactly."

Carter hung up and stumbled to the bar. He grabbed a glass and a bottle. He threw the glass against the wall and drank directly from the bottle.

Carter noticed the bottle was empty, and he dropped it to the carpet. He looked up as Joe Crifasi's chunky, fullback-type body moved through the bedroom door.

"You look damn near as bad as she does," Crifasi said, lighting two cigarettes and passing one to the Killmaster.

"At least I've still got feeling," Carter growled, accepting the long Italian cigarette and dragging deeply. "What's the verdict?"

"Knife got her jugular, first try. Whoever he was, he knew what he was doing. And . . . she was raped."

"Jesus." Carter crushed the butt.

"He took whatever report she was typing, but we might get a break."

"How so?"

"The typewriter was new, just issued. My boys think they can get something off the platen."

Carter nodded. At this point, anything would help. "They put people on Lockwood?"

Crifasi nodded. "Yeah, but I imagine they'll just faze him out. If the KGB knows we know, Lockwood would never be good bait now."

That clicked in Carter's brain. "Then it was a bad time for them to kill her."

Crifasi shrugged. "Could be a contract deal. The killer on the fringe not knowing what she was handling, just told to nail her and take anything pertaining."

"What about Bolivar?"

"Got people working. Without a specific area, it could take time. Can you remember any more about the three who worked you over?"

Carter closed his eyes and concentrated. "Not much. The little one was a boxer, very fast. The two big ones were just gorillas, but they were good."

"I'll put out feelers."

The doctor entered the room and Crifasi stepped aside.

"I can do more for you than for her," he said grimly. "Where does it hurt?"

"All over," Carter muttered.

"Take your shirt off."

Carter did, painfully, and gritted his teeth while the gray-haired man poked, probed, and prodded. "One broken finger, a couple of cracked ribs, and that gash above your eye needs stitches. Want a local?"

Carter shook his head. "Just hand me another bottle of scotch."

Taping, splinting, and stitching took nearly an hour. During that time they removed the body. Carter tried not to think what they would do with it. It would be dumped somewhere far out of the city. When it was found, it would look like a mugging and would be relegated to the hands of the local police.

A lousy end for a beautiful woman and a good agent. But pawns fall when the kings, queens, and knights make their moves.

At last the doctor finished. He packed up his bag and departed, leaving only Crifasi and Carter in the villa.

"That's about it, Nick. Not much more for you here. At least they won't get to use Lockwood."

"Yeah, but I lost her. Leaves a sour taste. Anybody inform the countess yet?"

"No. Thought you might like to do it yourself."

The Killmaster moved across the room on shaky knees and picked up the scrambler phone. The Contessa Beatriz Balaria picked up on the third ring.

"Bea, Nick Carter in Rome. Sorry about the hour."

The familiar voice came back with an edge to it. "That's all right. What is it, Nick? You wouldn't call at this hour if it could wait."

"Joanna Dubshek. We lost her."

A long silence. "She was good. It's too bad. Another six months and I would have brought her out. Did you salvage anything?"

Carter told her about Lockwood and what else Joanna

Dubshek told him before he left for Parmo's shop.

"At least that's something," the woman replied.

"Maybe, but a lopsided trade. Listen, Bea, they had her tagged. It was a contract hit, but they tried to make it look like rape and common murder. She was blown. Any hints?"

He could almost hear the woman's mind working on the other end of the line. "None," she said at last. "She was deep. I used her sparingly, and usually with at least two cutouts." Another long pause. "Hard to understand, Nick. I've got four, maybe five other people working in her area and a lot closer to the edge than Joanna Dubshek. It had to be some kind of a fluke."

"We might have something, a name . . . Domingo Bolivar. Ring any bells?"

"None, but I can make inquiries."

"Do that, Bea. I'll ring you back."

"I'm flying to Paris in the morning, and then on to New York. You have those numbers?"

"Yeah, I'll catch you."

Carter hung up. Crifasi was on the other line. He finished about the same time as Carter, and turned.

"The woman at the bar, Carmella . . . ?"

"Yeah?"

"One of my people asked her, real nice. She saw nothing, heard nothing, remembers nothing. According to her, she didn't even see you."

Carter nodded. "Figures. Don't blame her. She gets involved, she may get dead." He checked his watch. It was past four. "She would be gone by now."

Crifasi passed him a slip of paper. "I figured you'd like to ask her a few questions yourself. Want a driver?"

"I can manage."

Carter parked on the street. It was new, an enormous, sprawling complex of several buildings. He found the right building and took the elevator to the tenth floor. Carmella Perez lived in apartment D. He rang the bell. When that got no response, he knocked.

"Yes, who is it?"

"An old scotch drinker . . ."

"What?"

". . . come to cash in a rain check."

The door opened a couple of inches and her face appeared in the crack. "It is you."

"In the flesh . . . what's left of it."

"At least you look a little better," she said, and smiled.

"You look every bit as good . . . what I can see," he said grinning painfully.

She laughed and closed the door. The chain was dropped and it opened again, wide. "Come in."

He did, and kicked the door shut behind him.

Only a thin, togalike robe of sheer material stood between Carmella Perez and the world. Her skin was the color of coffee mixed with cream, her burnished auburn hair shined, framing her face and cascading below her shoulders. The light gleamed off her long, strong legs, the wide-curved hips and flat belly. Her body was proportioned except for her breasts. Braless now, they blew the hell out of the theory of gravity.

"Your face looks sore."

"My whole body is sore."

That was all it took. She took his good hand and led him into the bathroom and set him on the closed commode. Then she turned the water on full force in the tub.

"Nice place," Carter said.

"I get your meaning," she chuckled. "You're wrong. I own the club."

Carter nodded. "One of my people came around and asked you some questions."

"That's right. I told him nothing."

"I'm going to ask you the same questions."

She leaned forward and took his face in her hands. "You, I will probably answer. But later . . . after."

He sat where she had put him, listening to the water splash in the tub. Suddenly he didn't care about the three men. He was in her hands.

Gently she peeled him naked. She whispered several curses in Spanish when she saw his body. "Mother of God, what did they do to you?"

"In good old American English, they beat the shit out of me."

"I'll keep the water level below your bandage. Get in."

The warm water felt like heaven. The instant he hit it, Carter felt a gentle, seeping comfort, and sighed.

He wasn't surprised when Carmella cast aside the wispy robe and slid into the tub with him.

"The water," she murmured, "does it hurt you?"

"Some," he whispered back. "No matter. Heat draws out pain."

He was so big in the tub, large though it was, that it was a tight fit. They put their arms around each other and scooted closer. That was better, much better.

Carter couldn't resist. He snaked his hands down from her shoulders and gently hefted her breasts.

"You think I am a freak?" she asked, wide-eyed.

"No," he replied, "I am."

"You? What do you mean?"

"I've lasted this long without molesting you."

She laughed. It was a hearty, earth-mother laugh that echoed off the walls and made her whole body shake. "You think you're up to molesting?"

"I'm recuperating fast."

For the next hour they played, dawdled, and played some more. Then she helped him out and dried them both with several oversize, velvety towels. By the time she had finished them both, the floor was covered with damp towels.

"Bed?" She smiled.

"I thought you'd never ask."

The sheets were cool. Her body was warm and soft and yielding. All but the major aches and pains faded as desire took over.

They kissed, tentatively at first, then with quickened urgency and desire. She urged him to lie back on the bed.

"Let me," she crooned.

She came over him. Flesh met flesh. He caressed her slowly, firmly kneading and relaxing her shoulders, then let his hands slide down her throat to encompass her lush breasts, softly slipping the nipples between his fingers before bringing the pressure of his lips to bear upon them.

He couldn't seem to get enough of her earthy voluptuousness as he moved his powerful but gentle arms around her waist and clasped his hands to the small of her back, pulling her tightly against him.

For long moments they pressed their bodies together, breathing heavily under the impact of the fierce emotions that gripped them both. Carter's mouth opened hers, took hers, his kisses so tender and yet so demanding that she grew dizzy. She arched herself close to him, slid her arms under his shoulders, and molded her body to his, feeling as if they were sealed together. It was an excitement so intense that he could barely breathe, barely think.

A frenzy came over them. They tangled in a fierce embrace, arms and legs tight around each other, their demands almost violent now, totally beyond control. Carter's questing mouth, the feel of her satiny skin, the fragrance of her body, were like wild aphrodisiacs for him, driving him to passion.

Finally she guided him inside her, almost crying out as he took his first long, deep thrust. He drove deep within her, and her whole body quivered under the impact of this possession. He began the rhythmic movements of love, slowly at first, then with greater urgency, until at last they pounded together, each taking from the other, each giving, moisture running from their bodies, their breath coming in ragged gasps.

Before they were both ready, they both exploded together.

Slowly, they came down, still gripping one another in the aftermath. After several minutes Carmella rose and padded softly into the other room. She came back with cigarettes and scotch.

Sitting comfortably side by side in the big bed, they smoked and drank in silence. At last she rolled to her side and came up on one elbow.

"You are not police."

"No," Carter said.

"But you have power, friends."

"Yes."

"The little one took pictures, flash pictures, of you when you were unconscious."

Carter smoked in silence, mulling that over. They would be able to spot him now, but he didn't care.

"I know who they were," Carmella said.

He nodded. "I figured you did."

"What will you do with them?"

"Ask them some questions."

"And if they don't give you answers?"

Carter rolled his head to the side, letting his eyes meet hers. This was no ingenue. This was a woman who knew the score, had probably lived most of it.

"If they don't give me what I want," he murmured, "I'll kill them."

Carmella rolled to her back and stared at the ceiling for some time. When she spoke again, her voice was soft and her hand moved over to rest on his thigh.

"They are the Dobrini brothers . . . Guido, Carlo, and Daniele."

"Where can I find them?"

"I knew you would come, so I asked around. They have left Rome, but I know where."

"Where?"

"Will you take me with you . . . for a little while?"

"If you want to go."

"I do. They are in Naples. Are your bruises better?"

"Much," Carter said.

Gently, Carmella moved her big body over his, dropped her lips to his belly, and moved downward.

FIVE

Felipe Zapato fingered the telegram and read the text one last time:

> SAMPLE EXCELLENT. MY PEOPLE BE-
> LIEVE REMAINING MATERIAL WILL BE OF
> SAME SUPERIOR QUALITY. YOUR REQUEST
> AGREEABLE. PLEASE ACQUIRE WITHIN
> NEXT FORTY-EIGHT HOURS. WILL HAVE
> EVERYTHING WAITING WHEN YOU ARRIVE
> ALGECIRAS.

Fine, just fine, Zapato thought. Bolivar had taken three precious weeks to confirm the sample and give him the go-ahead for the job.

Now it might be too late.

The telegram had arrived at four that afternoon. He had picked it up and returned to the villa. The telephone call from the only man in the world he trusted, Alberto Ferare, the man who for years had fenced the jewels that Zapato stole, had come two hours before, at seven.

"Felipe, the word is on the street in Malaga and Seville.

47

The Guardia Special Force has your alias. It's only a matter of time before they narrow you down to the villa."

Immediately, Zapato had started a small fire in the fireplace. Papers, letters, notes—everything went into the fireplace. He dropped the telegram into the flames and sighed.

He would have to go into hiding now. It would be a week, two weeks, perhaps a month before he could return to Seville and the villa of Beatriz Balaria.

Damn the man Bolivar for his caution!

Outside, it was a hot August night. Crickets were alive in the garden and birds chirped in the trees. Now and then a bullfrog would croak from the pond near the walk.

Suddenly, all sound ceased. Nearby, his housekeeper's dog—a mongrel named Chico—lifted his head, cocked his ears, and emitted a growl from low in his throat.

"Mother of God," Zapato hissed under his breath, "they are here already!"

He had already changed his clothes and filled his pockets and a small bag with what he would need. He was ready to leave the house. He crumbled the ashes in the fireplace with his foot and went into the kitchen. His cook stirred a stew, staring into the pot now and then.

"Dinner?"

"An hour, señor, no more."

"I think I'll lie down for a moment. Wake me when it is ready."

"Sí, señor."

The dog was on alert, growling again, as Zapato moved through the living room and up the stairs. In the bedroom, he lifted a disguised section of the ceiling and crawled into the attic. It was hot, stifling, and he crawled to a rear window and peered out.

It was early evening, not yet full night. A shadow was out of place against the wall at the back of the garden, just inside the gate. He could not be mistaken. He knew every shrub in the garden.

The dog began to bark. There was still no sound at the front door. He turned to a side window, saw another misplaced shadow, and moved quickly to another window at the front of the house. They had it watched from all sides.

The dog was barking steadily by the time the doorbell rang.

Zapato had one path of escape open to him. It was not the easiest, but it would do. When he heard the cook's loose slippers slap across the floor as she went to answer the doorbell, he stepped out onto the roof where he often slept on hot nights, climbed the low railing, balanced himself for a moment, and jumped.

The man in the garden below heard feet scrape on the railing. Zapato, in midair, saw the white blur of an upturned face, and the dark blotch in it that was the man's open mouth. The man was too startled to shout, at first.

Zapato had never made the jump before, even in daylight. But he had thought about it many times, mentally measuring the distance, estimating the knee-spring that would be necessary and the swing to follow after he caught the branch of the olive tree. He had it all timed and precalculated in his arm and leg muscles. He could not see the branch against the dark background of the tree foliage, but it was there when he reached for it, flat out on his face in the air and stretching.

As his feet went down, he bent at the hips, kicked hard on the upswing, let go of the branch while he was still rising, and kicked.

Both his boots caught the Guardia agent full in the face. The man went down and a solid fist put him out.

Again Zapato went up the tree. At the very tip of a limb, he dropped silently to the ground and started off at a trot.

He ran through a vineyard that became a heavy grove of olive trees at the top of the hill.

Once, near the top, he paused and looked back. He could see lights going on in the villa. They were preparing to charge the bedroom. It would be several minutes before they broke down the door and discovered him gone.

It was a six-mile run to the coast. To be safe, Zapato stepped off the road into the trees when cars approached.

He had guessed right. Several fishing boats were just preparing to go out. He found one who, for the right price, was willing to put him ashore near Tangier, Morocco.

Zapato waited until land had passed from view before he crawled up on the wheelhouse roof and went to sleep.

It was about two hours before dawn when the old man shook him.

"Señor, my son will row you ashore here."

A half hour later, Felipe Zapato tipped the boy and jogged inland until he found a road. A passing truck gave him a lift into the city center. He waited in the market, eating breakfast and killing time until the sun was high, and then made his way into the Medina. It had been three years since he had been there, but it all came back within minutes. He found the number, opened a rear gate, and walked into a small courtyard.

In the alcove, a cat hissed at him and skittered out of his way. The door was slightly ajar. Zapato knocked.

"Who is it?" a raspy voice shouted.

"An old friend."

"I have no friends."

"Then an old enemy who needs lodging and will pay."

"Then come in."

Zapato pulled at the grimy handle of the door and walked inside. It was dark in the place, particularly after the brightness of the outside. Through the murk, he saw a dim figure sitting at a table.

"Felipe, what a pleasure! What brings you to Tangier?"

"Hello, Jean-Pierre. I am hot."

The old man shrugged his wasted shoulders. "Tangier is a good cooling-off place. How long will it take?"

"Two, perhaps three weeks."

Felipe Zapato felt his flesh begin to crawl as the stench of the room hit his nostrils and the small, shriveled figure rose to shake his hand.

"Twenty-five hundred francs a week and I'll throw in a bottle of wine a day."

"You are a thief, Jean-Pierre."

The sagging shoulders sagged even more. "Aren't we all? Take it or leave it."

"I'll take it."

"Good, good. Josette . . . Josette, you old whore, we have a guest! Coffee!"

A few seconds later a door opened and Josette Lamont entered. She was disheveled and wore a chenille robe that was in desperate need of washing. Her face was small and round, her features tiny. Atop a sharp nose perched a pair of thick glasses that magnified her watery eyes. Her hair—dull brown flecked with gray—was a mass of untidy curls. Her small hands were constantly in motion, fluttering like caught birds. She stared intently at Zapato, then asked brightly, "Who is it?"

"It's me, Josette, Felipe Zapato."

"Ugh," she grunted, and turned to her husband. "What is he selling this time?"

"Nothing," Jean-Pierre snapped. "He's buying . . . safety. Coffee."

She grunted again and filled two dirty cups. While the two men talked of nothing, she went to an upper floor and readied a room. A half hour later she was back.

"Room is ready. Top floor, on the right."

Zapato stood and stretched. He started to leave the room,

but was halted by one of Jean-Pierre's claws on his wrist.

"Forgive me, Felipe, but aren't you forgetting something?"

Zapato counted out the equivalent of twenty-five hundred francs in Spanish pesetas onto the table, and left the room. It was several minutes—not until they heard the upstairs door slam shut—before either of the couple spoke.

"Josette . . ."

"Oui?"

"Go over to the New Town and get me the latest papers from Malaga, Seville, and Madrid."

The old lady mumbled something about her swollen ankles, but she shuffled out into the sunlight.

Behind her at the table, Jean-Pierre Lamont slowly counted out the money, his lips spread in a grin over his brown, broken teeth.

Felipe, he thought, must have the hounds of hell on his ass. Either them, or the whole damn Guardia Civil!

Carter awoke alert but hurting. He could hear sounds in another part of the apartment and knew that Carmella was already up.

He groaned his way to the bathroom and splashed some water on his face. The man who looked back at him from the mirror was unrecognizable. He wrapped a big bath towel around his middle and re-entered the bedroom. Five minutes of slow, very careful, exercise gave him the courage to move farther than the confines of the bedroom.

The kitchen was huge. The floor was imitation flagstone, and a diverse selection of copper utensils hung from the ceiling and gleamed like a display of treasured spoils of war.

Carmella was standing next to the kitchen sink preparing grapefruit. She hadn't heard him enter. He leaned against the counter and observed her. She was dressed in only her underwear, and now, in the light of day, she looked even bigger than she had the night before.

He wondered how, in his condition, he had survived.

She glanced up and saw his reflection in the window. "Good morning."

"Morning. Do you always fix breakfast in your underwear?"

"Only when I have company," she chuckled. "Hungry?"

"I'll tell you after coffee."

He ran his fingers through her hair, which was still damp from a morning shower, and kissed her shoulder. "You smell good."

"Sit."

He did, over cigarettes and coffee. By the time the food was ready, Carter realized that he was starving. She sat, drinking coffee and watching him, not speaking until he had pushed the plate away and lit another cigarette.

"I sent your clothes out to be cleaned."

"Thanks."

"Your wallet, the gun, and that ugly knife are on the dresser."

"Did you look in the wallet?"

"Of course," she said matter-of-factly, and smiled. "You are some kind of American agent."

"Some kind," he agreed.

"The Dobrini brothers are very mean men. I have heard that even the dons of Sicily will have nothing to do with them. They are crazy, like animals."

It was Carter's turn to smile. "Then no one will mourn their demise, will they?"

Carmella shrugged and shook her head. "Then you are determined to go to Naples?"

"Yes."

"I make many phone calls this morning, to friends on the

street. The Dobrinis are in Naples, but no one knows where. They are, how you say, in the underground. But there is a cousin, Francesco Dobrini. He will know where they are."

Carter stood. "I wish you wouldn't come along."

"No, I have decided. I will go."

"Why?"

Carmella moved to him and crushed her breasts across his chest. "Because you may not come back, and I want to know you again, in bed, before you die."

An hour later they left Rome in her car, a sleek Mercedes, with Carter doing the driving.

Carmella knew Naples. She directed him to the Hotel Foria and the street of the same name. It was a good choice, a sprawling, many-pathed complex, fairly new, and a half-hour's drive from the congested center of the city. Carter guessed most of the clientele didn't stay more than an hour or two. There was a discreet and convenient outside entrance to all the halls leading to the rooms.

The concierge behind the desk was skinny, sleepy, pale, baggy-eyed, and bored.

"One night," Carter said.

"Eighty thousand . . . in advance."

Carter paid, signed the register as signore and signora, and took the key. The baggy-eyed man checked Carmella's chest, blinked, and jerked his thumb to the right.

"You go out, turn to the right, it's the second entrance. All the keys open the downstairs door, but it's individual keys for the rooms, and every room has an inside twist-lock. You're two-oh-two. It's a nice room, the best in the house."

They went out, turned to the right, found the second entrance, unlocked the door, trotted up a flight of stairs, opened 202, and it *was* a nice room. Air conditioning, wall-to-wall carpeting, a radio, television, a big double bed, and a tile-floored bathroom with a big tub and a stall shower.

Carmella hit the phone while Carter put on a dry shirt and changed the bandages on his face. She was hanging up just as he came out of the bath.

"He has an office in a building on the Tribunali behind the San Domenico basilica, fourth floor."

"What does he do?"

"He's a lawyer."

"That figures." Carter checked his watch. "Timing should be perfect. Let's go."

They cabbed to the Tribunali. It was nearly six o'clock, but the heat was still blistering when Carter guided her into the building. It had a false façade of marble, with a newsstand beside the lobby doors, a bar to the left with red neon signs, and beside its door was a business directory.

Carter consulted it. "Four-ten. Let's go."

They took the elevator up. The corridor was lined with frosted-glass office doors. A fire escape door stood open at the end of the hall. Carter checked it and returned.

The door opened into an outer office. Two desks were placed end to end, both sporting typewriters, telephones, and secretary paraphernalia. Carter pointed to one of them.

"Sit and play secretary," he whispered. "Somebody comes in, tell 'em the big man is gone for the day."

An inner door opened into a stylish office with leather and chrome furniture and a desk that dwarfed the young-old man standing behind it. He had a young face that contrasted wildly with a head of gray hair, and he was crawling into an Italian silk suit jacket that couldn't be touched for five hundred bucks.

"I'm sorry, the office is—"

"Francesco Dobrini?"

"Yes. Who are—"

"Never mind who I am." Carter was already at the desk

when the other man's hand dived into a side drawer. Carter's foot came up, slamming over the hand.

The howl of pain was ear-shattering, but it ended quickly when Carter's fist met spine through belly. Dobrini sailed across the room, spewing the linguini he'd had for lunch.

Carter picked up the five-hundred-dollar jacket and followed. He picked Dobrini up by the front of the shirt and cleaned him with the jacket.

"We're gonna talk, lawyer."

"My hand! *Mamma mia,* you broke my hand!"

Carter bounced his head from side to side until the bones in his neck were popping like champagne corks. When the man tried to kick him, Carter avoided it and stomped his other foot. Dobrini went down to the floor in a whining heap.

"*Basta!* Enough! . . . What the hell do you want? . . . Who are you?"

"You've got three cousins. They're here in Naples now. Where?"

"You crazy? You want to die?"

"I could ask you the same question, Dobrini. Guido, Carlo, Daniele . . . where are they?"

"Even if I knew, I wouldn't tell you!"

Carter thought of the silenced Luger and then a peeling job with the stiletto. But it would be messy. And he didn't think it would take that much to break this one.

Other than the door Carter had come through, there were two others. One was a walk-in closet with more expensive suits. The other was a rajah's bath, complete with a huge sunken tub and lots of marble.

The Killmaster grabbed Francesco Dobrini by his Gucci belt and the back of the neck, and dragged him into the bathroom. He lifted the lid on the commode.

"Where, Dobrini?"

"You son of—"

The rest was drowned out as his face hit the water. Carter counted and brought him up, gasping and choking for air.

"Memory better, Francesco?"

Sputter, sputter.

Down he went again, this time for a longer count. Instead of bringing his head back up, Carter flushed the commode. The water level went down low enough for Dobrini to breathe. He gasped, sputtered, and gasped some more. Then he saw the water level rising toward his face and screamed again.

Two replays of this, and he was begging. Carter pulled him out and dumped him on the floor. He lowered the seat and sat down, lighting a cigarette and putting his foot on Dobrini's neck.

Finally the man got enough air into his lungs to talk. "I don't know! I swear it, I don't know where they are holed up!"

"Hard to believe," Carter hissed, pressing a little harder with his foot.

"It's the truth! On my mother's grave, it's the truth! If they need anything, they call me here. If I need them, I page Signore Georgio Franconi at the Celebrite. It's a club in Capodimonte, just off the Corso di Savoia."

"Who's Georgio Franconi?" Carter asked, flicking his ash.

"It's the name Guido uses when he's traveling."

"Or hiding out."

"Yeah. Guido goes out to the Celebrite every night. He gets there around ten and stays until closing."

"Just to get your phone calls, Francesco?"

"No, no, it's the women. Guido's a freak. He's got to have it every night and he hates whores. Lot of factory girls go into the Celebrite. They work in the mills out there."

Carter leaned forward and blew smoke in the other man's

face. "Francesco, I'm going out there tonight and check this out. If I don't find Guido, I'm coming back here. And you know what I'm going to do?"

"Jesus, I told you . . ."

"I'm going to cut your balls off, lawyer."

The face went white and the lack of blood to the brain got him in seconds. Francesco Dobrini passed out.

Carter had him gagged and tied securely around the commode when he looked up and saw Carmella in the doorway.

"Is he dead?"

"Not so you'd notice," Carter said

"How did he get all wet?"

"He took a swim . . . in the john. You got a short skirt and a tight sweater with you?"

"No."

"C'mon, we're going shopping."

SIX

Guido Dobrini was whistling as he pulled off the highway and dipped down into the little village. The main body of the village was made up of little stucco shacks and old stone houses. Beyond the village was the tire factory, and beyond that the row of little cafés and clubs.

Between the point where the old village left off and the row of clubs began, there was an American-style motel that did a brisk two-hour business starting at midnight every night.

Guido guided the car past the motel and noticed the gas gauge: low. Right next to the Celebrite parking lot was a gas station.

Guido headed for it, shifting his little body in the driver's seat. It was still warm enough, even close to ten o'clock at night, to have sweated through his shirt so it stuck to the upholstery on the drive out from Naples.

Then he saw the woman. No, not a woman . . . a real live Amazon, standing on the edge of the parking lot when he pulled up to the pumps. He came to a sudden stop in amazement. He was looking at what Italian women were famous for and still he couldn't believe it.

His eyes might be gritty and strained from lack of sleep, but he caught the impact with more than mere eyesight.

"Completo, signore?"

"Sí. What is that?"

"That, signore, is incredible. She has been standing out there for nearly half an hour. Who knows?"

Guido Dobrini was spellbound. She wasn't young, but then she wasn't old either. The way she looked, it didn't make any difference. Her breasts were huge and perfect, outlined perfectly under the lightweight cotton sweater, which came down snugly over full hips.

Guido got only a glimpse of her face as she turned away, but he thought he had seen a look of pleading, possibly a look of fear, on the features. The woman's mouth was a shade too large for beauty, with its full red lips. but with her straight nose, big dark eyes under thick brows, and frame of auburn hair around her oval face, she was enough to stir him.

Her legs were, to his thinking, absolutely perfect. Not the slender legs of a model, but the lushly padded, gorgeously curved legs of a man's dream, the kind of legs a man yearns to press gently apart so that he can crawl between them.

Guido smiled. Why does a man, even a man who knows better, assume that lush outward beauty seems to promise sexual experience of unsurpassing perfection?

Nevertheless, seeing that picture of perfection move away, seeing the living bounce of those generous breasts, the achingly suggestive play of those unbelievable legs and the softly rounded buttocks above them, made him glad that he was alive.

He paid for the gas and crossed the area to the Celebrite parking lot. As he got out of the car he saw her again. She was by the canopied entrance to the club, and seemed to be asking a question with her eyes. She had the same look of appeal he had seen earlier and, with a barely perceptible movement of her head, was looking down the road. If she was asking for a lift, she was making certain that no one but he could know, and Guido, his heartbeat picking up sharply, nodded.

She was into the front seat in a second, and in the pale glow of the dome light, he could see the look of appeal now loosening into a smile. She pushed against him, the warm firmness of her thigh urgent against his.

"I don't pay," he growled. "I never pay."

"I just want some fun . . . a ride in your fancy car. Okay?"

"Okay," he said, smiling.

"Let's get out of here," she begged. "Right now!"

Elated, Guido started the car along the road. The adrenaline was churning silently through him from her touch. The incredible luck of having this lush creature wait for him made his muscles lurch with anticipation.

The shade of her legs, almost the same as the short brown skirt, looked like panty hose, but he tentatively laid a hand on the thigh next to him and got a happy surprise. She wore no hose, and the flesh was smooth and firm and very faintly damp. The skin was as soft as a baby's.

He flicked the overhead light on again so he could see her more closely. He expected to find some flaw . . . more age than appeared at a casual glance, some marks of coarseness and commonness, pehaps a dullness of expression. Not that he was that particular. In his present state, her gorgeous build and her readiness to get in a stranger's car were enough for him. A cinch lay, that was the main thing.

But she was every bit as beautiful as she had seemed, with smooth, flawless skin, lusciously formed lips, slightly tremulous now under his gaze.

She dropped her eyes and laced her fingers in her lap,

and he saw that her hands were small and delicate. He flicked off the light and replaced his palm on her thigh, and she laid her own hand on it in gentle welcome.

"I'm Guido." He slowed the car. "Where can we pull off the road?" he asked quietly. "We ought to talk."

Oddly, she giggled. "Suits me," she said. "If I get picked up, I figure I have to wrestle a little. Take that side road up ahead."

The break in the brush and trees wouldn't have been seen by anyone but a native. It led to a clearing fifty or sixty feet across, thickly strewn with empty cans and litter.

"Good," she said. "Nobody's here. Probably won't be, either, until after the bar lets out."

She turned to Guido with an unstudied willingness, and put her face up to his for a kiss, her open mouth sweet and rich, inviting his tongue, and either she was very warm by nature or a complete little actress, for she moaned immediately and wriggled closer against him.

Guido continued kissing her, but a slightly sour note intruded his mind. Was she the village whore? Incredible, with her youth and beauty—even a sort of innocence, strangely enough—and yet he had known prostitutes this young or younger.

To settle whether she merely meant to neck or was willing to spread her legs for him, he slipped his left hand between her thighs.

Her arms clutched even more fiercely around his neck, and she not only moved her thighs apart but also lifted slightly, so that his fingers slid immediately against the crotch of her panties.

Guido Dobrini sighed and kissed her even more passionately. This was definitely his lucky night!

Suddenly, the car door was opened and Guido was yanked out. He felt himself being heaved through the air, and then grunted in agony as his body was slammed across the hood of the car.

"We meet again, you little shit."

Guido Dobrini pushed the shock and the pain from his body and mind. He turned his head toward the voice and snapped open his eyes.

"You!"

"Me, bastard."

Dobrini's left arm was twisted up between his shoulder blades. When he recognized Carter, his free right hand went for the small of his back.

Carter smashed it, and pulled a silenced Beretta from under the man's jacket.

"You're gonna die for this," Guido squeaked, flexing the fingers of his right hand to restore some feeling.

Carter put the Beretta in his own belt. "Talk to me, Guido."

"Fuck you."

Carter's left hand was a vise around the little hood's neck. He balled his right into a fist and jammed it between the man's legs. The resulting howl of pain ended in a gasp.

"My guess is you and your brothers are free-lance. Who hired you?"

Dobrini tried to get his right hand between his legs to massage himself. Carter intercepted it and bent two of the fingers back until one of them cracked.

Another scream. But no words. The little fighter was tough and stubborn, but Carter had expected that.

"It doesn't make any difference to me, Guido, how long it takes to kill you. Now, you and your brothers worked me over after you beat the video man to death. Right?"

"That was an accident, I swear. Jesus, ease up, I can't breathe!"

"Who hired you!"

"I don't know. We get orders on the phone."

"Bullshit," Carter hissed. "Whoever killed the Polish woman needed help tailing her. *Who*, Guido?"

The little man's face was stark white and covered with sweat. But his jaw was set and he wasn't talking.

"You are scum, Guido, but I don't mind if you hold out. The longer you do, the better I like it."

Carter inexorably tightened the pressure on Dobrini's windpipe as he spoke, cutting off any sound except a faint, whimpering moan. At the same time, he moved the man's arm upward between the shoulder blades, inch by inch. The pain caused Dobrini's eyes to protrude while his face and body writhed and contorted in Carter's merciless grasp.

"I've got another guess, Dobrini. Whoever hired you killed the woman while you and your brothers were working me over. *Who*, Dobrini?"

There was an abrupt splintering crack as the elbow ligaments gave way. Carter let go with both hands and stepped back dispassionately to consider the groaning figure that flopped on the ground beside the car.

On the other side of the car, Carter heard a gasp and looked up. The woman was standing, white-faced, her arms at her throat, her wide eyes staring at Carter. The combination of the cousin, Francesco, and now Guido was too much for her.

"Move, back down the road," Carter murmured. "This isn't pretty, but it's going to get nastier."

Carmella swallowed hard, nodded, and moved away a good distance. Carter returned his attention to Guido, who had crawled to his knees and was cradling his broken arm, muttering curses under his breath.

"That's just one arm, Guido. I want a name and some particulars. I want you to point a finger or I start breaking them all, one by one. Then the other arm. Then I go to the legs . . ."

"All right, all right. Jesus, you're crazy."

"Just mad, Guido. Believe me, you haven't seen my crazy half yet." Carter stepped forward and cocked his leg for a dropkick.

Dobrini cringed. "No, no! Don't hurt me no more! I'll tell you! Mother of God, don't touch me again!"

He was huddled on the ground with his face in his hands. He began sputtering out words intermingled with sobs, and Carter had to lean close to hear more clearly.

"Lucchi. His name is Tony Lucchi. We know him from the old days here in Naples."

"Where is Lucchi now?"

Again the words became mush. Carter dragged the cringing man to his feet and flung him against the side of the car.

"Stop your goddamned sniveling and talk so I can understand you! Tony Lucchi. Where can I find him?"

"Spain, somewhere. I think Madrid. This is the first time he's been back in Italy in two, three years. He did some contract hits for one of them Red Brigade outfits and it got too hot for him. He went to Spain."

Good, Carter thought. That meant there was a chance that Interpol would have a line on him. Just in case, he asked and got a physical description, and more.

"He's mean, man. He looks like a kid, an angel, but he's weird. He especially digs cutting up women."

"I found that out," Carter growled. "Who pays him now?"

"I don't know, I swear—"

The heel of Carter's hand flashed out and ruined the man's nose. Blood mixed with the tears now, coursing down his face. His right arm was grotesquely twisted and he leaned far forward to hold it pressed tightly against his body in the angle between torso and limbs. He avoided Carter's gaze and moaned in agony.

"Do we have to start this all over again?"

"The Bear! When Lucchi gets in touch with him in front

of us, like on the phone, he always calls him the Black Bear. That's it, I swear it!"

"You swear a lot, Guido," Carter hissed, pulling out the Luger from his shoulder rig. "Now the jackpot question. Carlo and Daniele."

"No way! No way, you son of a bitch! I don't give you my brothers!"

"I'll find them anyway, Guido. You can make book on it." He cocked the Luger and set it on the hood of the car. "Just like the old Wild West, Guido, Go for it!"

"You're nuts."

"It's the only chance you've got, Guido."

The little man was sweating, his eyes darting from the Luger to Carter and back to the gun.

"Well, Guido?"

"It's a hunting lodge in the Vomero Forest called Silver Pines, just off the Via Rosa."

"Thanks, Guido."

Carter turned away and started walking. When he heard the scrape of the Luger across the hood, he pulled the Beretta and turned. Guido's face was pure shock when he pulled the Luger's trigger and nothing happened.

Carter fired from the hip, emptying the Beretta into Dobrini's chest. He crossed to the body, and after wiping his prints from the gun, dropped it on the man's belly. Then he picked up the Luger and took a magazine out of his pocket.

"Same chance you gave Eduardo Parmo, Guido," he growled, jamming the magazine into the Luger's butt and jacking a shell into the chamber.

He climbed into Dobrini's car, backed it around, and headed down the lane. Carmella was sitting on a tree stump near the main road. When Carter braked, she approached the car.

"Get in."

"Is he dead?" she asked, her voice hollow.

"Yes. Get in."

She did, and Carter drove the mile or so to the pullout where he had left her car.

"Drive back to the hotel. I'll meet you there in a few hours."

Her eyes were stricken when she turned to face him. "You said he was dead."

"Guido is dead."

"Then why . . ."

"There are two more. The brothers, Carlo and Daniele."

"My God, you're no better than they are!"

"Yes, I am," Carter said, not meeting her eyes. "I'm alive, they're dead. I'll meet you at the hotel."

Carmella crawled out of the car, crossed to her own car, and got in. The engine came to life and, without looking back, she drove away.

Carter waited until her taillights were completely out of sight before he pulled Guido's car into gear and moved out himself.

He made two stops.

The first, a construction site he had spotted off Corso di Savoia on the drive out. He parked in a grove of trees near the fence and used the limbs of one of them to get over the chain link and barbed wire.

The door to the explosives shed was steel, but the lock was a piece of cake. Ten minutes later he came out with twelve sticks of dynamite and caps. A nearby ladder got him back over the fence.

The second stop was at a bar near the city. He got change and called the Contessa Beatriz Balaria's number in Paris.

"Bea, Nick."

"God, you keep weird hours."

"And do weird things."

He told her of the events of the past few hours, and the probable events of the next few.

"The Black Bear," she replied. "Probably a code name. That might help. So far, my people have nothing on a Domingo Bolivar. I'll put out more feelers and ask some questions about Tony Lucchi."

"When do you leave for New York?"

"Tomorrow. I'll be there for two days, and then the next six weeks at the house in Monaco."

Carter chuckled. "You jet setters."

The countess laughed. "Have to keep up appearances, darling. Stay in touch."

"Will do."

Carter hung up, dived back into the car, and headed for the Vomero Forest.

The cutoff was marked by a small sign denoting the lodge. Carter took it and cut the lights. The road became rougher and rougher, hardly more than ruts and rocks. Eventually it widened, and Carter eased up behind two Fiat sedans.

He checked his pockets for spare magazines for the Luger, grabbed the dynamite, and slipped from the car.

In the distance through the trees he saw a faint light. It looked to be about a mile away, on high ground.

He stayed on the path until the building was less than a hundred yards ahead. There he paused behind a tall spruce and checked it out.

The lodge was really a two-story cabin with rough, half-log siding. It looked bleak and lifeless other than the dim glow of a single bulb through the shutters over a second-floor window.

Beyond the cabin, moonlight glinted off a large pond. It looked to Carter as if the water went right up under the rear porch. So much for escape that way, he thought, unless they went swimming. It was a hundred feet on both sides of the cabin to the trees. Another break.

Carter dropped to his belly. He crawled through the grass, wiggling and inching his way along. The cool dew of the night coated his clothes and exposed skin, but he kept the dynamite high to keep the fuses dry. He slipped around the side of the house by crawling through the bushes and tall grass that almost formed a kind of shield around the front of the lodge.

Somewhere an owl started to raise hell, and now he could hear faint music from that upstairs room.

He continued to crawl through the maze of shrubbery. The bright eye of the moon was partially covered by clouds, and Carter would wait until it disappeared for a few precious seconds before he inched ahead on his belly, commando style, closer to the wood fortress.

At last he got within ten feet of the house. Now there was just bare ground, without vegetation to cover his movement. He jumped to his feet and ran until his back was against the layered half-logs. Carefully, he edged along the wall to a window. He peeked into the living room, which had glass doors opening onto a deck overlooking the pond. The room was empty, and the window was unlocked. He slid it up a foot.

He moved around the house in the opposite direction to a window at the other end—kitchen, pantry to the side, door open leading to a small dining room. This window also opened easily.

He broke the dynamite into three bundles and fused them. Gently, he slid one bundle into the kitchen window and then a second into the living room window. He scurried around the house and placed the third in the struts under the decking.

Carefully, he moved back to the trees in front of the lodge, playing out the fusing behind him. Then he twisted them together.

His lighter flickered and then caught. He shielded the

flame with his hand and lit the bound fuse. In seconds it split into three and burned its merry way toward the lodge.

They would go in sequence, kitchen first, living room second, deck third, about ten seconds apart. The initial fuse to the kitchen would take about three minutes.

Carter stood at the edge of the trees bathed in moonlight. "Carlo! Daniele!"

The light went out at once and the shutter cracked open.

"Who's there? Who's out there?"

"That you, Carlo?" Carter said.

"Who wants to know?"

"You don't know my name, but you know my face. You took a picture of it last night in Rome."

Just in time, Carter saw the barrel of a rifle poke through the crack, and he dived into the trees. The slugs hit tree limbs and shrubs several feet behind him as he scrambled in the darkness.

"Carlo, Daniele, whoever . . . you're a lousy shot!"

Again the rifle cracked. There was a tinkle of glass from the smaller window to the left, probably the bathroom, and three rapid pistol shots rang out in the still air.

Carter had already moved. He checked his watch: a minute and a half.

"Listen, both of you. You've got about a minute to get your butts out of there before I blow you up."

"Carlo!" came the voice from the shuttered window. "There he is over to the right!"

Again the pistol shots and the high-powered whine of a rifle. Bullets thumped against tree trunks or ricocheted and screamed away. Pine cones fell. Pine needles wafted down. But none on Carter. He was twenty feet away.

"Guido's dead. You hear me? Come on out while . . ."

They didn't hear the rest. The kitchen blew. Ten seconds later, the living room went.

The sky was lit with an orange fireball. Pieces of burning wood, glowing red and yellow in the black night, floated down from the sky.

Then the deck went, taking the whole rear wall of the lodge with it.

Carter crouched low at the edge of the trees. He set the Luger by his leg and pulled a cigarette from his jacket. He lit up and watched the lodge burn.

The cigarette was half gone when the rear of the roof crashed into the burning pyre.

Suddenly the front door opened and a man with a pistol emerged, rubbing his eyes. "Where are you, you son of a bitch!"

"Over here, Dobrini," Carter called, grabbing the Luger and coming to his feet.

The man moved out, letting the screen door slam behind him. Carter raised the Luger.

"I got him, Carlo! I see him!" The man raised the pistol and got off two wild rounds at Carter.

"You must be Daniele," Carter growled. "Good-bye, Daniele."

The man took two of three shots in his chest. He fell, rolled over, and lay still.

Then the last Dobrini, Carlo, appeared in the door behind the screen. The rifle had been replaced with a machine pistol, and he started spraying.

Carter moved to the side and forward, the Luger jumping in his outstretched hands. Ten feet from the porch it went dry and he jacked in a fresh magazine.

The porch screening shredded. Carlo dropped the machine pistol. He hit the screen door, tore it away from its hinges, and tumbled across the porch and down the steps to roll, facedown, at Carter's feet.

Carter flipped the body over with his toe. Several of his

slugs had been high. Carlo Dobrini wasn't recognizable anymore. His face was beyond any semblance of humanity.

The Killmaster holstered the Luger and trotted back to the car.

Carter eased the door open and slipped into the room. Immediately he was on the alert. It was too quiet, not even the sound of breathing.

Tensing, ready to spring, he flipped on the light.

One look told him everything. The bed had been slept in but was now empty. Her bag was gone.

He found the note in the bathroom, stuck in the edge of the medicine cabinet mirror:

Nick, or whoever you really are,

I know you will be reading this because I know that the Dobrinis don't have a chance.

The one night with you was like no night I have ever known. Now I know why: you're forbidden fruit. I couldn't handle another night knowing what I know now. I know this sounds silly, but it sounded like an adventure when we left Rome, like something you read but don't believe.

Well, when I saw you with Guido, I believed.

I thought I had seen everything, and if I hadn't seen it, I'd heard about it. Or I thought so, until I met you.

Thanks for the first night. I think it will take me a lifetime to forget the second.

Carmella

Carter rummaged through his bag until he found a pint of Chivas. He took it to a table by the window and sat. He drank, read the letter again, and then burned it.

Then he drank some more, and thought, and stared down at the lights of Naples.

What had she expected? What had he expected she would expect . . . that was more like it.

He was used to it. But did he really have to do it . . . all three of them?

An hour later the pint was finished.

"Yeah," he said aloud, moving to the phone, "I really had to do it."

It took three calls to find a sleepy Joe Crifasi.

"It's done. The three of them. I'll need some quiet transportation out of Naples back to Rome."

"Where are you?"

"Hotel Foria, two-oh-two, on the Via Foria."

"I'll have a car there in twenty minutes. Are you staying in Rome for a while?"

Carter hesitated.

"No, I've got to get back to my own kind."

"Huh?"

"Nothing. Get me on a plane to Nice. I'm meeting the countess in Monaco in a few days."

SEVEN

Each day, Josette had brought the papers. He wasn't getting front-page coverage, but the coverage he was getting wasn't dying out.

Felipe Zapato called Alberto Ferare.

"I've got a score, Alberto, a big one."

"Where are you?"

"In Tangier, with Lamont and his wife."

A groan. "Felipe, that pair would turn you in for anything they can get."

"I know. Jean-Pierre follows the papers every day. He knows I am not cooling off. I've been here a week and already he has upped the cost twice. I'm running out of money and I have to get back to Spain."

"Now? Good God, Felipe, you'll never get past the frontier."

"Let me worry about that, Alberto, old friend. Can you lend me some money?"

"A little . . . I'm sorry, Felipe. Like you, the cops are putting many of the old guard out of business."

"Five thousand, American. It spends easier here."

"That much, yes. Will you use François?"

"Yes, I have already contacted him in Casablanca."

"I'll have the money to you in the morning."

The next morning, Zapato met a small, dark-haired woman in the coffee shop of the Hotel Salazar. They sat together in the same booth, chatted, drank coffee, and she left, leaving a thick envelope in Zapato's lap.

He took the bus to Casablanca, and by midafternoon he was sitting in the shop of François Sauze.

For years, Sauze had been an acrobatic clown in the Grand National Circus of France. He was a genius with costume as well as makeup, and there was little he could not to with his lithe, supple body.

But Sauze plied an even more lucrative trade in the dark of night when he would leave the circus. In his day, François Sauze was the most accomplished thief in the world.

Eventually, a smart insurance investigator put the circus together with the crimes and Sauze was caught. He was tried, convicted and given thirty years.

He got out in twenty and fled France for Morocco. Now he did odd jobs for old friends, exchanged a bit of money, and ran the costume shop.

If anyone could change Felipe Zapato's appearance, it was François Sauze.

"How radical do you want it?"

"Very," Zapato replied. "Completely. As you can see, I have already started growing a beard."

"Yes, good. We'll make it a Vandyke and gray it. Also, I have fillers. They fit over your back teeth and add pounds to your face. There is a dentist here who can do the work. Blue contact lenses will take care of the eyes. Also, when the time comes, we will shave here and here . . . give you a forehead. Come into the fitting room."

Zapato spent four hours in the fitting room. It was agreed that he would need a full wardrobe, including at least three suits and a body brace that would keep him perpetually stooped and add age. The suits themselves would give him fifty extra pounds around the hips and waist.

At last they finished and agreed on the price. Zapato paid him in full, including the cost of a new passport.

"How soon?"

"Five days, a week at the most."

Zapato took the bus back to Tangier and made his way into the Medina. Lamont's house was dark. Zapato thought it odd at that hour, but entered anyway.

The musty cubbyhole of a living room was empty. Jean-Pierre Lamont was not in his usual chair. There were no sounds of Josette in the kitchen.

Years of instinct took over, but not quickly enough. There were two of them, one at each inner door. They didn't have their guns drawn, but each of them slapped leather-covered saps into their palms.

"Felipe Zapato, you are under arrest in the name of the king. Extradition arrangements have already been signed for you to return to Spain."

Over one of the policemen's shoulders he saw Lamont's grinning face.

"Watch him. He's a tricky devil, fast like the wind."

The door was out. Zapato backed toward the courtyard window. "Jean-Pierre, may your rotten soul roast in hell for this!"

"Let it," the old man cackled. "I'll enjoy the reward while I'm still living. Watch him, I say."

The two policemen made their move a fraction too late. Felipe Zapato grabbed a footstool from the floor, held it in front of his face, and dived through the window. He took the fall like an acrobat, hitting with his shoulder and rolling. With the same agility, he went up and over the courtyard wall. He landed running on the other side, with shouts and blaring whistles behind him.

He scrambled over another wall into another courtyard.

He grabbed a black djellaba, still damp from a clothesline, and went over another wall. He ran down an alley, pulling the djellaba around him. Slowly, the sounds of the whistles faded in the maze of the Medina.

But he knew he was far from free. Already he could hear the blare of sirens. They would be hurrying to cover the gates that separated the old Medina from the New Town. His only chance was to somehow blend with the throngs going through the walls.

Every doorway he passed seemed to hold questioning eyes. Not too fast; make haste slowly. There were other pedestrians around and he adjusted his pace to theirs while trying to ignore the growing sensation between his shoulder blades, his ears ready for the cries that would stop him, followed by the bark of the volley of bullets.

When he reached the corner he could bear it no longer, and as he turned, he risked one long look behind him before the wall intervened. Prophecy again. Burned on his retina was an image of someone pointing down the street in the direction he had originally taken, while uniformed figures rushed past him like hounds upon the scent.

A false scent. Now he had to muddle his trail some more while he considered what he should do next. The squeal of protesting brakes sounded in his ear as a battered bus stopped at the curb to disgorge passengers.

In an instant he was in the midst of pushing figures with baskets, dangling squawking chickens, bags of beans, crates of cucumbers. This wave rushed away and a minor backwash of passengers streamed past to board the bus.

It was natural to join them, and Zapato swept in, to fumble out the coins in payment and to stand, surrounded and lost in the crowd, as the vehicle rumbled away.

What next? For the moment he was safe, but the haven was only a temporary one. He searched for an answer but could find none. His mind wasn't working too well; the affairs of the previous week and the resulting fatigue were taking their toll. For the moment it was all he could do to hold to the smooth metal of the pole and jounce along with the other passengers.

What to do next?

The rest of the passengers decided for him as the bus ground to a halt one last time. There were shouts of instruction and the wild clucking of suspended hens as everyone exited, Zapato as well, carried along with the press of people.

When he was outside and had managed to force his way clear, he saw that they were in the open-ended cavern of a bus terminal. A sign with a list of cities was picked out in red letters against the dirty white of one wall, but they were distant and hard to read.

What was close was a rumbling giant of the road, tires as high as his shoulder, with a winding line of prospective passengers snaking toward its open door. Without further thought, Zapato joined the end of the line and others grouped up behind him.

They had shuffled forward a few paces before he realized that all the others held tickets, no doubt purchased inside the station. This was not a good thing. He liked the idea of boarding this bus at once, wherever it was going, though he disliked immensely the idea of asking for a ticket, being surveyed by the agent who would undoubtedly be a man of suspicious manner and keen memory who would later tell all he knew to the police.

What could he do?

The man ahead of him, a farm worker in simple clothes, clutched his cardboard ticket between work-gnarled fingers. Zapato leaned forward and spoke quietly into his ear.

"Friend, I am late arriving here and very tired. Would you save me the inconvenience of buying a ticket at the window by allowing me to purchase your ticket from you at a price twice the sum printed on its face?"

"Done," the man said without a moment's hesitation. Money and ticket changed hands, and the man hurried away to buy a second ticket.

The quick transaction went unnoticed in the crowd. A moment later and Zapato was aboard, taking one of the few remaining empty seats next to a woman of solid girth whose ample flesh lapped over onto his cushion, as did her armload of packages.

"Excuse me." With his solid flank he pushed at her gelled one until it jiggled aside and gave him room to sit down. The flank's owner sniffed loudly but said nothing.

Within the minute the door closed, to the cries of the outraged ticket holders who could not be jammed in, while the barking exhaust of the bus echoed from the concrete walls and into the street.

Safety, for the moment, lay with motion, and Zapato sighed inwardly. Then he realized that there was still one important point he was unaware of.

"Would you tell me where this bus goes?" he asked his seatmate.

She first delivered a look that made silent comment on his sanity or the quantity of alcohol he had recently consumed, and only after this message had been delivered did she reluctantly answer the question.

"Casablanca."

"Thank God," Felipe Zapato said with a sigh, and leaned back in the seat.

Two days later, in the cellar under Sauze's shop, Zapato saw the article in the society column of the Seville paper: *The Contessa Beatriz Balaria has let her Seville villa, Balaria, to French screen star Monica Verraine during the*

shooting of Señorita Verraine's new film in the Seville area.
The contessa will take up residence for several weeks in
Monaco . . .

"Shit," Zapato hissed, "just shit. François . . . François!"

"Mon Dieu, Felipe, what is it?"

"Tomorrow, I must leave tomorrow!"

Zapato's mind was racing. The countess would inevitably
take her most valuable possessions with her to Monaco.
That meant the books would be with her. His passport and
disguise would last for only a limited time. He would need
as much time as possible to case the villa in Monaco.

"Tomorrow, eh? It will cost extra, Felipe. I will have to
bring the dentist in all night, and I will need at least two
extra seamstresses . . ."

"How much?"

Sauze thought. "A thousand."

Zapato squeezed his temples. That would leave him only
two thousand for the job.

It would have to do.

"Done."

At eleven o'clock the next morning, a Moroccan rug merchant named Mohammed Omed—a fat, stooped man with a
graying beard and dull blue eyes—walked up the gangway
of the Greek cruise ship *Olympic Star*. Two days later the
ship would make a port of call in Nice, France.

EIGHT

The casino was crowded with glittering, bejeweled women and tanned, tuxedoed men who seemed to ooze money instead of sweat from their pores.

But one woman outgleamed all the others. She had skin the color of cappuccino, and a beautiful, exotic face with high cheekbones and flaring nostrils. Her lips were full and crimson, her almond eyes so smoky, so languorous and challenging that every man in the room who saw her couldn't help but stare.

An hour earlier, when she had swept in with her entourage of admirers and friends, conversation had stopped at the sight of the extraordinary-looking, seemingly Oriental woman. The blue silk gown she wore clung sensuously to her perfect body, its low, scooped neckline revealing jutting, flawless breasts.

Those in the room who didn't know were soon told that this was the wealthy and exciting Contessa Beatriz Balaria.

And the rumors flew.

But Nick Carter, at the bar at the far end of the room, knew the truth.

She was born Beatrice Regis in Tokyo, the daughter of

a marriage between a wealthy Japanese film star and a British professor of English and French in the occupation schools of Tokyo. She was an absolute beauty, a true beauty, but she was much more. From her mother she had learned how to pamper men exquisitely, and from her father she had learned perfect English and French.

Carter knew all about her, because in intimate moments she had told him.

In Tokyo, at seventeen, she had won a beauty contest, and from that moment had become determined to go to Europe. Upon reaching her maturity, she had. And in Paris she had developed into a high-income showgirl. She was nineteen and the toast of Paris when she met an aging, wealthy count, Luis Balaria of Seville. A week later they were married, and Beatrice Regis became the Contessa Beatriz Balaria. She learned fluent Spanish along with her French, English, and Japanese, and gave the old count new life . . . for a year.

He went like he wanted to, in bed.

Next came a retired Texas billionaire named Gordon Nash. He adored Beatriz, and in the four years they were married made her one of the richest women in the world.

Gordon Nash also died in bed.

There were two more husbands, who all got as much as they gave and died happy.

Somewhere between husband number three and husband number four, the countess came to the aid of Carter and AXE. It was an intricate mission that couldn't be executed without someone of her worldwide influence. When it was over, the countess had found a new calling.

Now, in her late thirties, she had no husband, though she still used the title of Contessa Balaria despite her subsequent marriages. Her empire expanded—she had homes in Paris, Monaco, Seville, and New York—and she had pursued her secret calling until she was the control of the largest spy network in Europe.

Idly, Carter sipped his drink and checked out the countess's current entourage for the evening.

There was the ballerina, Natalia Mydova, radiant, young, and innocent in a plain white dinner dress, her hair drawn back severely from her lovely face.

An American couple, the Kinkaids. Harvey Kinkaid, who had made his fortune in California real estate, had retired at an early age with his wife to a hilltop château in a suburb of Nice. The Kinkaids were regular visitors to the casino, had lost enough money there to indicate they could afford more, and were well known on the Côte D'Azur for their lavish parties. It was at those parties, whose guests included much of the international set, where the countess did much of her recruiting.

The second couple was Herman and Helga Butz. Butz was a West German steel industrialist who did a huge business with the Soviet bloc. He was a dark-skinned man in his sixties, a serious gambler and a system player. His wife, twenty years younger than he, was a handsome, full-bodied woman who liked to flirt. She played baccarat or sat at the roulette tables with no real interest in the game. Each evening, her beautiful dark eyes would roam beyond the cards or the spinning wheel until she caught the attention of some man.

Her flirtations were innocent enough, a look, lowered eyelids, another look, a half smile, a little turn of the shoulder, another half smile. It was all quite harmless, and it infuriated her husband, who grew paler and more tight-lipped as it went on, glaring first at his wife and then at the uncomfortable object of her interest, until he could bear it no longer. Bursting with suppressed rage, he would take his wife away from the game.

Such were the people who constantly surrounded the countess. Sometimes they would unknowingly give her information; sometimes they would lead her to a recruit. But always they supplied her with a cover.

They were all gathered now around the chemin de fer table. Carter waited until there was a vacancy at the table, then he sidled through the ropes surrounding it.

The countess looked up as he sat down, not the slightest sign of recognition in her eyes. "Oh, new blood. Welcome, monsieur."

"Madame."

"I am the Contessa Balaria."

"Simon Gordon."

"Ah, an American. I love Americans. They are so reckless with their money."

The other players introduced themselves, Helga Butz skewered Carter with her eyes, and the shoe went to her husband. He placed a 20,000-franc chip on the felt and turned to Carter on his right, who had the first choice as active player.

Carter calculated quickly—20,000 francs, approximately $2,500—and matched it.

"Banco," Carter said.

"Bravo," said the countess, and sipped her drink.

The German scowled, his wife, to Carter's right, rubbed her knee against his, and the deal began.

The object in chemin de fer is to draw a number of cards that total as close as possible to nine. Aces count one. Ten and pictures count zero. Other cards count by their own rank numbers.

Butz slid one card from the shoe to Carter and the second to himself. A third to Carter and the last to himself, all face down.

Carter casually examined his cards, a five and four. He flipped them over.

"La Grande."

Butz snorted and passed the shoe.

Carter played carefully and his luck held. At 20,000 francs, he amassed another $15,000. After a while he lost a coup to the ballerina, who lowered the stake to 5000 francs and quickly lost herself.

For the next hour, Carter made small bets against the bank, winning some, losing some. During this time he swapped witty repartee with the countess and encouraged Helga Butz's eye-lowering advances.

Eventually Butz could take it no longer, threw his usual tantrum, called his wife a tart, and dragged her from the table.

A few hands later, the ballerina grew bored. She stood, kissed the countess on the cheek, and excused herself saying that she would see the countess at her villa for a pool party the next day.

That left Harvey Kinkaid and his wife, who played as one.

Carter bet lightly until the Kinkaids had the shoe. When this occurred, he made sure he matched or overbet the active player. The Kinkaids' losses were heavy to that point, so they were doubling and tripling their bets to recoup.

The Killmaster, as best he could, counted the cards that had been played. This was difficult since there were eight decks shuffled into the shoe. Difficult, but not impossible.

The circumstances were just right when his turn came again as active player.

Kinkaid had won four times in a row. If he stayed with his method of play, he would gamble big on his fifth attempt. He evidently thought that a hot run would always go to five. If he won the fifth with the bank, he would drag half his winnings and start over again.

He played true to form, placing ten 20,000-franc chips in front of the shoe, approximately $25,000.

Face cards, tens, and combinations of eights and nines

had been rampant the last six draws. The shoe was low, about fifteen cards left. That meant the bulk of the fifteen were low cards. Both of the next two hands would most likely come close to a combination of eight, *La Petite*, or nine, *La Grande*.

"*Banco,*" Carter said, and matched Kinkaid's pot.

When the four cards were dealt, Carter held his look with an unexpired breath until Kinkaid had looked, dropped his cards, and glanced up.

Only then did Carter exhale. The man did not have a combination of eight or nine. Carter checked his own cards: a queen and an ace. Since the queen was zero, he had a count of one.

"*Carte,*" Carter said.

Kinkaid dealt face up and smiled. It was a seven. From Kinkaid's point of view, Carter was probably over nine. He shook his head, declining a draw.

Carter flipped the ace and queen. "Eight."

"Seven," Kinkaid said, flipping his own cards. "Congratulations, Mr. Simon. My dear?"

The Kinkaids left the table. That left nothing but strangers with Carter and the countess. She waited a few hands before calling, "*Banco.*"

On the countess's first hand against Carter's bank, she held a seven. The Killmaster purposely did not declare an eight, and the countess had the bank.

From there on it was easy for Carter to constantly outbid everyone for the bank. It was also easy to draw or hold in such a way that the countess, inside an hour, had broken him.

"You are far too lucky, madame," he said, rising. "I believe I will call it a night."

"I believe it would be unsportsmanlike not to offer you a drink and breakfast," she said with a warm smile.

"I would be charmed."

And so to the casual onlooker, the countess had made a tidy sum and the tall American had made a conquest.

No one thought differently as they strolled from the casino arm in arm.

Carter whistled to himself as he tooled along behind the countess's chauffeured limousine. He felt at ease as they climbed into the hills above Monaco. Few people would ever suspect that their meeting was anything more than the beginning of an affair between two attractive and obviously wealthy people. Such things happened every day on the Riviera.

The sleek black car turned between two brick pillars into the driveway of an enormous three-story villa. Out of habit, Carter checked along the road fore and aft, and wheeled in behind the limousine.

Manicured green lawns, cascades of flowering vines, and brightly colored flower beds attested to professional landscaping. The house itself was a symphony of white stucco and glass. It was a little Spanish, a little Moorish, and a little French, contrasting markedly from the traditional Riviera architecture they had driven past moments before.

Carter parked, got out, and beat the chauffeur to the rear door. As he helped the countess out, his hand giving her arm a familiar squeeze, he leaned forward and whispered in her ear.

"Servants?"

"Three," she said. "No one new."

To cement her words, Carter checked the chauffeur and remembered the bulldog face. Ditto with the manservant who opened the door and nodded.

"A pleasure to see you again, monsieur."

She led Carter into a huge great room furnished in white and gold, the yellow tiled floor ·lotted with handwoven white rugs, the walls hung with costly abstract oil paintings.

"This way."

It was a small, book-lined study with two sections of a wet bar cleverly concealed into both sides of the fireplace.

"Would you like a drink first?"

"First?" Carter asked.

The countess chuckled. "Before we go to bed, *cheri*. We can't disappoint the gossipers at the casino, now, can we?"

Carter accepted the drink and they both folded into a large sofa.

"I have a little information on Tony Lucchi, a great deal on the Black Bear, and nothing on Domingo Bolivar."

"Give me what you have," Carter sighed.

"The Bear is a code name, obviously. He has operated for years in Spain and Morocco. Evidently he is powerful enough to deal directly with Moscow. When they need something, anything, he can set it up. Assassination and blackmail are his specialties. He operates free-lance, but his leanings are definitely toward the Communist party. He has quite a reputation, Nick, and he is as elusive as hell."

"Anything that would hook him to Bolivar?"

She shrugged. "I don't know yet. The key seems to be, find Bolivar. The name is obviously an alias, and whoever he is, he keeps a very low profile. I should know more, perhaps all, by tomorrow night. Natalia Mydova is working on it for me."

Carter's head snapped up. "The ballerina?"

The countess smiled. "Natalia defected with the help of the KGB. What they didn't know was that I had recruited her long ago."

"Okay, but if Bolivar is the Black Bear, and he's so tight with his security—"

She held up a hand. "That is covered. Natalia will request assistance in Spain. That is being set up now."

"Good enough. Now about Tony Lucchi."

"A very, very bad boy." She rose and walked across the room, her body's movements under the dress creating thoughts in Carter's mind far afield from business. She lifted a tiny piece of molding, pushed a hidden button, and a four-by-four section of the bookcase slid upward. Behind it was a safe. "Would you give me a hand?"

A few quick twists of the dials and the safe was open. Inside, Carter spotted several jewel boxes, some stacked bonds, and other paraphernalia the rich would keep in their safes.

She walked to a nearby television set, picked up the remote control, and dialed numbers. From the safe Carter heard a click.

"Flatten your hand on that side and pull, gently."

He did. The inner lining of the safe slid out, revealing another safe just behind it. Seconds later that safe was open and the countess had extracted two sheets of paper. When both safes were resecured, they returned to the sofa.

"That will give you everything I have found on Tony Lucchi. When you have read and digested it, our business will be done for the evening." She stood and lightly brushed her lips across his. "I will be waiting in my suite. It is the second door on the right, third floor."

She rustled from the room and Carter read.

Anthony Lucchi had had an illustrious career in his native Italy. He was suspected of kidnapping, payroll robbery, extortion, and more than one murder. He had only been indicted once. That was for the murder of a prostitute in Milan, but the case had been thrown out of court for lack of sufficient evidence.

A psychiatric report on Lucchi was frightening, but it hadn't been enough to hang him. If the report were accurate, Lucchi was definitely a psychopath, particularly when it came to women.

There had been six identical murders—in Milan, Rome,

and Naples—within a period of three years, with Lucchi as a suspect. But nothing concrete had ever been proven.

Carter noted sourly that the killing of Joanna Dubshek was similar.

Three of the women and two men killed during the same period were closely identified with radical left-wing organizations. Each of them had been on the verge of arrest or cracking when they were killed.

The information Carter read gave him little doubt that, if Lucchi was the killer, he had been hired to shut these people up. The other killings were probably random, just to feed his psychotic needs.

Lucchi currently had an apartment in the Prosperidad section of Madrid, and a house off the Ramblas in Barcelona under the alias Raphael Santo.

There was a photograph. Carter studied it, and felt a twist in his gut. Lucchi was in his early thirties. In the picture, he looked a good ten years younger, and the face smiling up at Carter wouldn't hurt a fly.

So much for appearances, Carter thought grimly.

He burned the report, pocketed the photograph, and climbed the staircase to the third floor, mulling over in his mind how he could get Tony Lucchi and the Black Bear at the same time.

He knocked and entered. The countess was by a huge canopied bed pouring champagne. The way she looked drove all thoughts of Tony Lucchi from Carter's mind.

She glanced up, smiled, and did a pirouette. "Like?"

"I like."

"It's a Boldonni creation."

It was a lavender jump suit, and a creation it was, for many reasons. First, the fabric. It was see-through, gauzy as a veil, cleverly transparent but absolutely sturdy. Why it simply didn't disintegrate was one of the reasons it was a creation. Another reason was the cleverly cut body stocking that came with it. Worn with the body stocking, it was daring, revealing, but decent. Without the body stocking, it was daringly revealing and deliciously indecent.

She didn't wear the body stocking, but did wear the thin chain belt that was the third and last part of the ensemble. The metal belt had many links, but it was so conceived that it modestly hid the navel, and that was the only important part of her that was unexposed.

Carter accepted the glass. They toasted silently, and then talked with their eyes.

The glasses were set aside and she deftly, with a minimum of movement, shed the jump suit.

"Am I still beautiful, *chéri*—" she murmured.

Carter swallowed her naked perfection with his eyes and groaned his answer.

Her hair, thick and glossy, hung several inches below her shoulders. Her entire body was in perfect proportion. Her breasts were firm and round, the nipples tilted slightly upward. Her waist was tiny, blossoming into hips that were properly broad. Her belly was no more than a gently rising mound. Her legs were long and beautifully shaped.

He took her in his arms and mashed his lips to hers. His breathing had quickened and he uttered a soft, urgent moan as he felt her tongue meet his. The feel of her naked flesh rippling beneath his fingers as she pressed herself to him was electrifying, sensuous.

He groaned as he felt himself swept into the familiar desire. With one motion, he picked her up and carried her to the bed. He stripped off his clothes and they came together with the burning need of animals. She writhed under him, hot and moist, her softness, her lush breasts, and her pounding hips an equal match for his own desire.

"Too long," she moaned.

"Far too long."

As he titillated her with his fingers he leaned forward and kissed the tip of one of her breasts. She reached out, urgently caressing his head and shoulders. Her hands combed through his hair and she curled tendrils of it around her fingers. She bent her head down and began kissing him, running her lips over the side of his face and ear.

"Let me do it," she said softly. "You lie back and stretch out your legs." He did as he was told. She raised herself to a crouching position over him and lowered herself. He watched her face in fascination. She closed her eyes and parted her lips, which were glistening with dampness. Her eyelashes fluttered as she moved her hips from side to side, driving him into her.

He lifted his hips and she gave a small, choked cry as he completely entered her. She stayed absolutely still, her eyes tightly closed, breathing through her parted lips. Then she let out the pent-up breath with a long, luxurious sigh and pressed herself downward. He stroked the tips of his fingers along the inside of her thighs and across her stomach, as he began moving upward with firm thrusts. The rocking bed and its ryhthmic sound added to the sensuality of the moment.

She lifted his chin and began kissing him hotly on the lips, repeating his name over and over. He reacted, pushing himself upward with unrestrained movements. She responded eagerly. He gripped her waist in his powerful hands and began lifting her. The muscles covering his shoulders and arms stood out in hard relief as he arched his body into hers. They kept their frenzied pace until she began emitting an intense groan of pleasure.

He rolled her beneath him in one smooth motion.

"I'm close, so close," she whispered.

Carter closed his eyes and concentrated so that he could

catch up with her. Soft, fluttering sounds escaped her lips like butterflies. He gritted his teeth as he raced to meet her head-on.

"Don't stop, Nick, please don't stop!"

Suddenly she was a dervish of desire with her panting gasps and cries, her fingernails clawing at his back. Then he climaxed in a sweet sharp burst of fire. Hearing her deep moans, he knew that she did the same.

NINE

The next morning, back in his own rooms at the Hotel de Paris, Carter showered slowly, enjoying the laziness of it. He was well rested, his mind alert, his body fully recovered from the pummeling it had taken. He luxuriated in the thick Turkish towel that he used when he stepped from the shower. He shaved leisurely and carefully, taking an almost sensual pleasure in the act.

The ball was in the countess's court now, and it was probably better that it was. If he poked around trying to connect the Bear with Bolivar, he would only draw attention to himself and perhaps lose the element of surprise. Better that the countess and her minions do the legwork so that when it came time to go, the Killmaster went direct.

He ordered breakfast from room service and dressed at a leisurely pace: golf shirt, light slacks, and deck shoes. By the time he finished, the food had arrived and he sat down to fresh-squeezed orange juice, sausages, scrambled eggs, croissants, and strong, steaming coffee.

He ate with relish. Everything was right with the world.

And then the telephone call came.

"Hello?"

"Good morning, Monsieur Simon. I trust you enjoyed the evening?"

Carter chuckled. He recognized the countess's voice. "It was worth every penny."

"Then I hate to rain on today's parade." The change in tone was drastic.

"Problems?"

"Several. I think it best that you don't attend my little pool party this afternoon."

"Oh?"

"Perhaps a swim at Cove's Reef, beyond San Remo. Do you know it?"

"I do."

"Good. The lady in question will be swimming there as well. Shall we say noon?"

"Noon it is," Carter said, and the line went dead.

He hung up and moved out onto the balcony. It was a pretty day—blue sky, clouds white and fluffy—but suddenly all Carter could see was gray.

Felipe Zapato, stooped in the clothing and harness of the rug merchant Mohammed Omed, strolled the sunbaked promenade above the Cove's Reef beach. He was hot, his shirt stuck to his back, and he envied the seven-eighths-naked vacationers sporting on the strip of beach below the promenade. They swam or dived, or sprawled on the sand, coloring the beach with brief bright bathing suits and tanned bare arms and legs.

The beach in midsummer, Zapato thought with a sigh, was no place for a man who had to wear clothes. He would give anything at that moment to be lying on the beach with a chilled glass of wine in his hand and no troubles.

Then he saw her . . . tall, long, dancer's legs, her dark hair tied at the nape of her swanlike neck. She wore a teal blue, very brief bikini beneath a short beach jacket.

It was going to work, Zapato thought. Following her from the countess's villa had been a stroke of genius.

He watched her walk from the dressing room cabana to the edge of the water. She shed the jacket and pulled on a white bathing cap over her dark hair. When she waded into the water and struck out for the diving platform anchored a hundred yards out, Zapato turned inland from the promenade.

Quickly, he walked to the parking lot and retrieved his car, a rented Volvo sedan. In seconds he had swung the car around and drove to the private parking area. He paid the fee and charged up the lines of cars until he spotted the little Mercedes convertible. The top was down with a cardboard shield over the two bucket seats.

Zapato sighed. The space to the right of the Mercedes was empty. But then it should be. No one wanted to park in a space littered with the glass from two wine bottles.

With a small whisk broom and a paper bag, he cleaned up the glass and pulled into the space. Then he sat for a few moments making sure he wasn't observed.

When he was sure of himself, he jumped from the Volvo and ran around the Mercedes. One quick tug and he released the hood latch. Another scan. No one. Deftly he flipped the generator clips and lifted the top. The rotor came off easily. He cracked it, replaced it, and set the top back down and clipped it.

When the hood was down and locked, Zapato strolled back to the promenade.

Natalia Mydova reached the raft with sure, powerful strokes and pulled herself up. Tugging the bathing cap from her head, she shook out her hair and scanned the beach and the rocky arms that reached out on each side from the sand into the sea.

Almost immediately she saw the dark head she was seeking only a few yards from the raft, heading her way from the side. Two hands curled over the raft, and as she watched, the body of a man came up onto the raft, the water streaming smoothly from his powerful, bronzed body.

Natalia returned his nod, averted her eyes, and lay back. She heard him sigh and stretch out on the other side of the raft.

"Why all this?"

She slid her hand under her bikini and withdrew a photograph in a watertight bag. "This, for one thing." Idly, she flipped it across the raft.

Carter opened the seal and examined it. The photo was of him, out cold, and it was only too clear where it had come from and who had taken it.

"Does that picture tie you to Joanna Dubshek?" she asked.

"Yes."

"Then you know why we can't be seen together. And of course you realize why I cannot be seen going into Spain with you."

"Of course," Carter said. "I'm sorry. Did I compromise the countess last night?"

"No, we don't think so. That photo was only distributed to *rezidents* and field agents this morning. Instructions were to watch and report."

Carter let out a low whistle and shielded his eyes from the sun's glare. "Do you have anything else for me?"

"Yes. It was a risk, but I put through a request for help in southern Spain. I used the excuse that I have charmed an American senator who will be there next week on an inspection junket of military bases. I asked for a direct courier for my information."

"And . . . ?" Carter asked, holding his breath.

"I was given a cutout number in Seville. The contessa and your people were set up. I called the number, gave them my code name, and asked for the Black Bear. They asked for a number where I could be reached, and told me I would be called back in one hour."

Carter had heard the routine many times before, but he mumbled his understanding and told her to go on.

"When the call came, we managed a trace."

"Seville?"

"No," she replied, "Algeciras. The call came from a dead-drop relay line in an office on the Calle de Sesto."

"Shit," Carter cursed.

"Wait," she chuckled. "The office was checked. It is empty. But there is an importer in the same building by the name of Domingo Bolivar."

"Christ," Carter said, "you mean they couldn't find him before if there is a Domingo Bolivar?"

"Monsieur Carter, there are probably twenty-five Domingo Bolivars in every city in Spain. We had to narrow it down. Besides, *this* Domingo Bolivar is also a local politician, high up in the maritime office. By working for the Spanish government, he was left off all the usual lists."

"Sorry again," Carter said, and concentrated for several moments before speaking again. "Even now the only connection we have between the Black Bear and Bolivar is a dead-drop phone relay."

"I am afraid so," she replied. "But at least it is something."

"Yeah, something."

"You will go?"

"Of course I'll go."

"They might be watching for you to enter Spain. After the deaths of the Dobrini brothers, they might guess you know about Tony Lucchi."

"I can handle that."

"There is a woman named Dolores Martinez. She runs a maritime insurance agency. The contessa has already contacted her. She will aid you in any way she can."

"Thanks. And give my best to the countess." Carter stood and walked to the edge of the raft. "Take care of yourself."

"You do the same, Monsieur Carter."

He dived cleanly into the water and swam with powerful strokes toward the rocks from which he had emerged.

Natalia Mydova watched him out of the corner of her eye. She waited for another twenty minutes, then swam back to the beach. No one gave her a second glance as she picked up her beach robe and walked into the dressing cabana.

Ten minutes later she was in the parking lot heading for her car. The air was stifling now, but it didn't bother her. The relief of having this dangerous meeting over made her feel good. Too good.

"*Bonjour, mademoiselle.*"

"*Bonjour.*"

The graying, stooped man with the toed-out walk turned into the space beside her and opened the door of a gray Volvo.

Natalia got into the Mercedes and turned the key. Three times she tried the key, and the car would not start.

"*Pardon, mademoiselle.* May I be of some assistance?"

It was the old man. He had stopped his Volvo behind the Mercedes, and now his sagging, sad face was leaning over the door toward her.

Natalia sighed. "Not unless you're a mechanic."

His arms came up in a helpless gesture. "I am so sorry. I am a rug merchant. I am afraid I know nothing about automobiles." He handed her a card.

"Damn," she hissed, and stomped from the machine.

"But I notice a French tag on your car, mademoiselle. I am returning to Nice. Perhaps I could drop you somewhere along the way and you could notify a garage to pick up the car."

• • •

Zapato played the kindly old gentleman to the hilt. When Natalia begged to be let off in Monte Carlo to take a cab up into the hills and the villa, he would not hear of it.

By the time he swung the Volvo through the gates of the villa, Natalia knew the life story of the rug merchant Mohammed Omed, and she was laughing at his amusing anecdotes.

The party was in full swing by the pool, so it was practically impossible not to invite the old gentleman inside for at least one drink. It was the least she could do.

The rug merchant met Contessa Balaria and several of the other guests, charming them all. So much so that the countess was amused rather than shocked as he moved around the pool handing out his cards and drumming up business.

The countess was used to picking up strange people on the Côte d'Azur. It added to her image of eccentricity. She dispatched two servants for Natalia's Mercedes, and mingled with her guests.

For two hours, Felipe Zapato drank and talked and mingled. No one noticed the many times he excused himself, pleading a weak kidney and the bladder of a child.

During these many visits inside the villa to *la toilette*, Zapato located the alarm system, each entrance and exit to the place, and the sliding bookshelves in the study shielding the safe.

At last he searched out his hostess.

"Madame, thank you for a wonderful afternoon. In my business I travel so much and it gets very lonely. You have brightened my day."

"Nonsense, monsieur. I thank *you* for coming to the aid of a lady in distress," the countess said, smiling graciously.

"*Oui, monsieur*," Natalia added, "*merci beaucoup*."

"*Bonjour*."

The two women watched the old man walk laboriously to

the Volvo, climb in, and drive off.

"A funny old man," Natalie mused.

"Yes," the Contessa agreed, "and quite charming."

Zapato waddled into his hotel room and dived for the telephone. Alberto Ferare answered on the third ring.

"It's me."

"Felipe, where the hell are you?"

"In France, Nice."

"Nice? I thought the score was in Seville."

"It's been changed. Alberto, I need a lookout, a woman, someone young, fairly attractive."

"The lover's lane routine?"

"Exactly."

"When?"

"I want to go tomorrow night."

"Good God, Felipe . . ."

"I must. The target will be at a yacht party. There will be only one servant in the house, an old cook. I might never get a chance like this again."

"Give me your number there. I will call you back as soon as I can."

"Thank you, Alberto. You won't regret it. You can take a year off on just the commission."

Zapato gave him the hotel and room number, and then redialed.

"Yes?"

"Señor Bolivar, please."

"Speaking."

As per his instructions, Zapato recited his room number and the hotel number, and hung up.

Nervously he smoked and paced for twenty minutes until the phone rang.

"Hello."

"Felipe, I have found someone."

"Thank you, Alberto."

"Go to the Forum Plage. Ask for Lucie. She works there, a beach girl. I have already made the contact for you."

"She has worked before?"

"Many times, Felipe. Good luck."

"Gracias, amigo."

Five minutes later, Bolivar called. "I take it, Señor Zapato, you are ready to move?"

"Tomorrow night. I will leave right from the job. Where can we make the exchange?"

"Let me think . . . you are in Nice?"

"Yes."

"This is Thursday. I will meet you Sunday evening in the bar of the Hotel Roc in Andorra. That will be best for both of us."

Zapato sighed with relief. "An excellent choice. You will bring cash?"

"Of course, señor. That, too, will be best. Until Sunday."

TEN

The airport at Perpignan near the Spanish border was small. It was also out of the way enough so that there was a very slim chance of it being covered. The border itself would be another thing, but if all went well, that would be taken care of by Joe Crifasi.

The head of AXE in Rome had been cut free to work with Carter for the duration of the mission.

In the terminal, Carter headed directly for a bank of phones and dialed the special number in Madrid.

"Go ahead," came the stocky Italian's raspy voice.

"It's me, Joe. How're we doing?"

"Tony boy is still here in Madrid. He hasn't moved except to hit a discotheque for a few hours every night. I think he's between jobs. We've got taps on the phone and his mail covered every day. *Nada*, so far."

"You've got the Barcelona house covered?"

"All the way. You still coming in?"

"If I've got transportation," Carter replied.

"You do. His name is Marc Lapin. He's bringing across a load of wine tonight. He'll stop by a place called Bar Diablo in Canet-Plage about ten tonight."

"How will I know him?"

"Dark glasses, dungarees, and T-shirt that says, 'When in Rome . . . get laid.' Just in case, he'll also be drinking Mexican beer."

"The T-shirt your idea?"

"Hell, yes," Crifasi said, laughing. "See you tomorrow."

Carter hung up and hit the cabstand. "Canet-Plage . . . a decent hotel."

A half hour later he checked into a decent two-star and paid for a week in advance. If anyone was asking, they would never expect that.

After dumping his bag, Carter hit the promenade and found an all-purpose beach store. He bought a small bag, swim trunks, and a towel, then went back to his room.

Carefully, he unpacked and hung everything up neatly except for a clean shirt, jeans, and the deck shoes. These he stored in the beach bag along with Wilhelmina and Hugo.

The clothes in the closet belonged to Simon Gordon, who would soon disappear.

Then he changed into the trunks, draped the towel around his neck and, beach bag in hand, hit the beach.

Forum Plage was at the end of Avenue Gambetta. It was one of several sections of the beach franchised to a local entrepreneur but open to the paying public.

Felipe Zapato paid his fee and walked on through the dressing room without changing. On the pebbly beach, he looked around at the occupied chairs and umbrellas and the idle paddleboats. A beefy beach type lounged against a row of unrented chairs, but Zapato saw no young woman.

And then she was there, in front of him. *"Bonjour, monsieur. May I help you? My name is Lucie."*

"Yes, a chaise, please, and an umbrella."

She scurried away and returned almost at once balancing

a chair under one arm and a beach umbrella under the other. She seemed oblivious of the fact that he was about to sit on the beach fully dressed.

"This way, monsieur," she said.

Zapato followed and waited while she set up the umbrella, cursing under his breath.

Damn, I said young and attractive, but not this young!

She was nineteen or twenty, and very pretty. She had the straight nose and heart-shaped face common to many French girls, widest at the level of the eyes and tapering to a delicate mouth and chin. Her hair was a short mop of blond curls, and her figure was still the figure of a young girl, slim and small-breasted. Her skin was golden brown from the sun.

"There you are, monsieur."

"Merci," Zapato replied, creasing a fifty-franc note around one of his cards and pressing it into her hand. "And a bottle of beer, Spanish, if you have it."

Her forehead furrowed and her eyes narrowed as she searched his face and fingered the note and card in her hand. At last her lips curled into a faint smile. She nodded and hurried away. Zapato slumped onto the lounge chair and masked the worry on his face with an open newspaper.

She returned and dropped into a crouch beside him to pour the beer. Her eyes were intent on the beer and the sunbathers around them. Her lips barely moved when she spoke. "When will you need me?"

"Tonight, for a dry run," he replied, looking straight ahead at the paper rather than at her. "We go tomorrow night."

"What time tonight?"

"Ten," he said.

"Shall I come to your hotel?"

"I'll be glad to pick you up."

"No, it will be better for me to come to your hotel, I

think. Where are you staying?"

He told her, and quickly outlined what would be expected of her. "Now, as to the price . . ."

"Seven thousand francs, cash, tonight."

"It is more than—"

"It is my price. I told Monsieur Ferare. Yes or no?"

She might look young, Zapato thought, but she thought with maturity. Quickly he did a mental calculation. Her fee would practically strap him, but there was nothing he could do about it. The job would be far too dangerous without her.

"Very well, we have a bargain."

She smiled and squeezed his arm. Immediately the eyes grew wider and the smile broadened. The rock-hard bicep beneath the thin jacket did not belong to a frail old man.

"Until this evening, Monsieur le Voleur."

Before he could rebuke her for calling him a thief out loud, she stood and jogged toward the concession stand.

The exterior of the Bar Diablo was like any other bistro along the promenade. It was big, noisy, and catered to everyone from teen-agers to retirees who baked on the beach by day and sought any entertainment by night.

There were three large trucks parked along the curb within a block of the place. They were all enclosed and unmarked, so it was impossible to tell which one went with Marc Lapin.

Carter entered. The place was packed. All the better, he thought.

The left wall and the center were filled with tables. Booths were in the rear, and the entire right wall was occupied by a red vinyl and chrome bar.

Carter hit the end of it and ordered a beer. With a cigarette in one hand and the beer in the other, he put his back to the bar and took a closer look at the room.

It didn't take long to spot Lapin. The T-shirt was like a

beacon. Carter waited a few minutes and sauntered over.

"*Bonjour,* Marc—it is good to see you again."

"Ah, and you, monsieur. Please, sit, sit!"

Carter dropped into the opposite chair and they talked until those around them paid no more attention. At last they both leaned forward and spoke in lower voices.

"You need to be in Figueras by two in the morning, correct?"

"That's right," Carter replied. "There is a small airfield just south of the city."

"I know it. The agreed price is five hundred—American."

"Done," Carter said.

"I must warn you, monsieur, that is Catalan country. The Communist party has eyes everywhere. You must do exactly as I say."

"I am in your hands."

Lapin sprinkled bills on the table and left. Carter wandered back to the bar and finished his beer. Ten minutes later he was outside, ambling along the sidewalk toward the three parked trucks. Lapin signaled him from the first vehicle.

"In the cab, monsieur, quickly!"

Carter dived into the cab and over the seats. A steel panel had been removed. Without being told, he crawled into the cubbyhole. Lapin's face appeared behind him.

"One rap means quiet, two raps—all clear. Three raps, pray. I will see you again in Figueras, monsieur."

The panel was rescrewed in place, and Carter forced the tension from his muscles. Once he was relaxed in the confined space he let the sway of the truck loll him to sleep.

She arrived on the dot of ten dressed in a dark blouse, jeans, and sneakers. Zapato let her in, checked the hall, and closed the door.

"Would you like a drink?"

"No."

"Good," he said. "Let's go to work."

For the next hour he laid out in detail, using a map of the area around the countess's villa, all that was expected of Lucie. When he was finished he went through it again.

"Do you understand?" he asked.

"Everything."

"Then tell it back to me."

She did, verbatim.

"Good. Let's go."

In the car, Lucie drove, while in the back seat Felipe Zapato removed his padded clothes, the wedged shoes, and the harness. The facial disguise he left in place, but he did remove the wig.

The narrow road wound through the hills about five hundred yards above the villa. It was dotted every four hundred feet or so by cutouts for motorists with automobile trouble. At night these were used as parking places for lovers to look out over the lights of Monte Carlo.

Lucie pulled into the one selected by Zapato and parked. He came over the front seat in dark trousers and a black turtleneck.

"Your face is the same," she chuckled, "but your body has lost thirty years."

Before he could answer, another car—a convertible with the top down—pulled into the space beside them. Zapato tugged Lucie into his arms and mashed his lips to hers. She responded at once, curling her arms around his neck and emitting tiny but audible growls of desire from her throat.

As they became more heated, Zapato heard a groan of despair from the other car, and they backed out.

"Good," he said, breaking the clinch, "very good."

"Yes, it was."

He ignored the remark and started winding a rope ladder around his middle. "This is only a dry run, but we'll treat it as the real thing. Talk to me!"

"If a light goes on anywhere, I honk once. If a car comes through the gates, I honk twice. If a car pulls in here and does leave, I play prostitute and ask them if they would like kinky company."

"And if they don't leave?"

"I leave, and meet you below at the cul-de-sac."

"Excellent. And if the police come by?"

"I lift the hood and tell them my boyfriend has gone for a garage man."

"Good," Zapato said, nodding. "Time?"

"Five past midnight."

"I'll see you at one sharp. If not . . . ?"

"I pull out and meet you on the promenade by the Forum Plage."

Without another word, Zapato slipped from the car and moved like a shadow down the hillside. One hundred yards above the rear of the villa, he dropped to the ground at a ten-foot chain-link fence overgrown with ivy and topped with barbed wire.

The night was dry and warm, with a soft breeze blowing off the sea through a clear sky. It made a rushing noise over his head, whipping the scrub brush of the hillside and slightly bending the trees. A hanging light across the road from the villa danced on its pole, casting shadows back and forth across the top two floors.

The stars overhead were bright, but the thin, fading moon would not rise until just before dawn. It was the kind of night Zapato liked best, and if the weather report was correct, the next night would be the same.

He grasped the ivy and tested his weight. It would hold three of him. Up and over he went, dropping into a crouch. Twenty steps took him to the retaining wall above the swimming pool.

Again he dropped to his belly to recon the house. The

light on the pole made a tinny creaking noise as it swayed. An automobile came up the road from the village below. It turned into the gates.

From above, Zapato heard a horn sound twice. He nodded in satisfaction. Lucie was alert.

He heard laughter from the front of the villa. A car door slammed. The front door closed, and the car rolled back through the gates and down the hill.

Moments later a light came on. Third floor, guest room, he thought; that would be the ballerina.

A chimney blocked that room's view of the pool.

Zapato dropped the rope ladder and scurried down it. In seconds he found the conduits from the main box in the wine cellar up the side of the house and through the wall to the alarm system.

He crouched by the conduit and laid out tools from his utility belt. He counted off three minutes. That would be the time it would take him to bypass and deaden the alarm system the next evening.

This done, he moved to the darkest corner of the house and, like a leech, attached himself to the old-fashioned clay drainpipe. Two minutes later he was on the roof directly over the west wing guest quarters. He crouched by a chimney, and for the next twenty minutes visualized himself going through the motions inside the villa. Finally he sighed with satisfaction.

With only the one servant there the next evening, it would be a snap.

At five minutes to one he retraced his steps, and at one sharp he slipped into the rear seat of the Volvo. The door was barely closed before Lucie started the engine and pulled out.

By the time they were at the rear of her house, Zapato was once again dressed as the rug merchant.

He rolled over the seat as she stepped from the car.
"Tomorrow at the beach?"

"Yes," Zapato nodded, and drove off.

He hit the Promenade des Anglais and drove just five
miles over the speed limit until he was across the Pont du
Voe. There he speeded up to exactly sixty miles an hour
until he hit the village of Cagnes. Just across from the town
square, he pulled into an alley behind a BMW motorcycle
shop, and checked his watch.

It was exactly two hours from the time he had gone over
the fence behind the countess's villa.

It took only a two-minute stop to drop Carter off near the
fence of the small private airfield south of Figueras. There
he crouched in tall shrubbery until the sound of the truck
had faded in the distance.

It was just past five in the morning, the soft hour before
creeping dawn. In the quiet, Carter surveyed the field. The
only lights came from the mouth of a single hangar and the
small cubicle above it that served as air traffic control limited
to daylight takeoffs and landings.

Carter scaled the fence and ran in a crouch toward a line
of four lightweight aircraft tied down in the shadow of the
hangar.

Halfway there, he spotted the number he wanted on a
twin-engine Cessna.

Seconds later he was in the cabin behind the rear seats
and under a pair of canvas engine covers.

For nearly an hour he remained hidden, wanting a smoke
but not daring to do more than move now and then to adjust
his weight.

It was shortly after dawn when he heard voices and felt
the fuselage sway as the wing-tip-to-ground tie-downs were
removed. Shortly after that he heard the clamor of the pilot,

and then the twin engines came to life. As soon as the engines were warm, the plane taxied out. A little gibberish over the radio and they were rolling.

Two minutes later, Carter heard the pilot call his name over the muted roar of the engines. He pushed the canvas aside, sat up, and stretched.

"You might as well sit up here until we hit Malaga." Carter crawled forward and dropped into the copilot's seat. "Sandwiches and a bottle of wine in that bag."

"Thanks," Carter said, extending his hand. "Nick Carter."

"Emmanuel Lorca. Señor Crifasi sends his regards and said to tell you Madrid and Barcelona were still quiet."

"How long until Malaga?"

"Two hours, give or take."

Carter lit a cigarette and opened the wine. As he smoked and drank, he thought about Domingo Bolivar, and hoped he could get information out of the man before he killed him.

The countess would really like to know how Joanna Dubshek had been blown.

ELEVEN

The sun was high by the time they landed in Malaga. Carter had no trouble finding the battered blue Peugeot in the parking lot. He pulled out immediately and hit the coast road south toward Algeciras.

It was a two-hour drive and he didn't push it. At San Roque, a village just up the coast from Algeciras, he pulled off and found a telephone.

The number he had been given was answered at once by a youthful and bored female voice.

"Señorita Martinez, please.

"Who is calling?"

"Rodolfo from Madrid."

"One moment."

It was more like ten seconds. Carter heard another phone picked up and a click as the first one was replaced. The voice that came on was husky and no-nonsense.

"Where are you?"

"San Roque."

"Driving?'

"A blue Peugeot, beat-up, licence 4D3-909."

"Take the inland route. Come in from the hills on the

road from Medina. Leave now. You should arrive on the outskirts of Algeciras in a half hour. I'll be driving a white Mercedes two-door." The phone went dead.

Carter climbed back into the Peugeot and took off.

The back roads were small and poorly marked, but he managed to come out on the Medina road in twenty minutes. He cut left and saw a sign: ALGECIRAS—8 KM.

Six kilometers later, a horn barked behind him and a white Mercedes shot around him. Carter speeded up and fell in behind the car.

Five minutes later they hit the town and began zigzagging through back streets and back alleys. Suddenly the Mercedes swung left into an open garage. There was space for another car, and Carter took it.

He had scarcely killed the engine, when the door behind the two cars dropped, dipping the interior into darkness. He stepped from the car and sensed her right beside him.

"This way. Watch your step."

He followed. He heard keys. A door opened into a small, equally dim laundry room. Another door opened and they stepped down into a tastefully decorated living room. A few steps into the room, she turned to face him.

"Welcome to Algeciras, Señor Carter."

She was tall, with short black hair and a model's figure in a clinging yellow dress. Her arms, shoulders, and legs were slender, but the rest of her curved in and out in all the right places.

"Thanks for the help," Carter said.

"Would you like a drink?"

"I'd kill for one."

"No need," she chuckled, moving to a sideboard. "That bedroom will be yours while you're here. You look like you could use a shower."

"I could."

118

"Go ahead. The clothes you ordered are in the bureau and armoir."

Carter thanked her again and moved through the bedroom directly into the bath. The shower felt like heaven. He was shaving, a towel wrapped around his middle, when she pushed the door open and entered.

"Your drink."

She placed it beside him and sat on the commode. She sipped from a glass of wine and spoke.

"I've got Bolivar's routine, which he adhere's to daily, and his place of residence. He lives well, a villa near Tarifa above the sea."

"What's his background?" Carter asked, alternately sipping the drink and scraping his face.

"Clean. And I mean *very* clean. If Bolivar's the Black Bear, he has managed to hide it very skillfully."

"That's a tall order," Carter growled, "if he's got his fingers in so much."

"So far, I've come up with nothing that would tie him into the Russians or the local Communist party."

"Except the phone in the other office."

She laughed. "Everyone in Spain is doing a shady deal or two these days. Truthfully, I don't think that proves a thing."

"Can I go through the office?"

"I shouldn't think it would be too difficult to arrange."

"And you've got his routine?"

She nodded and closed her eyes in concentration. "Every workday, he leaves his villa at ten-thirty, arrives in his office at eleven sharp. He works until one-thirty, then goes across the street to a sauna. There he sweats, gets a massage, has a light lunch, and takes a short siesta. He returns to his office at five. He works until nine, and returns to his villa."

Carter dried his face, picked up his drink, and moved

119

into the bedroom. She moved right behind him, and it was several seconds before she became aware of the awkward situation.

"Oh, you want to dress."

"Uh . . . yeah."

"Dress," she said with a throaty chuckle.

Carter shrugged, dropped the towel, and began to dress. "Any further word on my photograph?"

"Nothing solid, but by now I'm sure you've been identified by Moscow."

Carter strapped the Luger to his leg and nodded. "That's almost a sure thing, so the quicker I can get things done, the better. Where would Bolivar be right now?"

The woman checked her watch. "It's almost two, and Friday. He'll be at the sauna."

"Then he'll be there until five."

"Always," she said. "He never varies."

Carter was dressed now and combing gray into his temples. A salt-and-pepper mustache almost completed the picture. He turned to her for the rest.

Without being asked, she handed him a pair of midnight-black wraparound glasses and a red-tipped cane.

"Also, here are two snapshots I managed to get yesterday with a zoom lens when Bolivar came out of his building."

Carter glanced at them and slipped them into his pocket. "They'll help."

"The address is Fourteen Calle de Sesto. You can get a cab two blocks south of here."

He nodded. "Stay by your phone. I told Crifasi I wanted reports every hour or so on Lucci in Madrid."

The Killmaster tapped his way down the front stoop and turned left. At the corner he hesitated, and a pretty young girl grasped his arm.

"Watch your step, señor. There is a gutter runoff there. Let me help."

"Bless you, child," Carter rasped, and allowed himself to be guided across the street.

Domingo Bolivar stood naked in the stall shower and let the ice-cold water wash the sweat from him that the sauna had raised.

He felt good today, especially good. By eight o'clock this evening, the deal of a lifetime would be completed. At nine, with any luck, he would lock his door, and by Monday he would be on his way to a six-month vacation in Brazil.

He deserved it. He had worked hard for twenty years to take such a trip. If he locked up this deal this evening, he wouldn't be a rich man, but he would be a financially comfortable one for the rest of his life.

At Domingo Bolivar's age, the specter of the coffin was shimmering imminently. But he was still strong and healthy, and ready for lots of play and very little work. And that was what he planned to do.

Wrapping a towel around himself, Bolivar retired to his private cubicle and called for the masseur.

He was rubbed with aromatic oils, pounded and kneaded, bathed again in hot water, showered in cold water, and vigorously curried with thick towels.

After a light lunch, he retired to the small cot for his siesta.

Carter paid off the cab two blocks from the building and tapped his way to 14 Calle de Sesto. Inside, he barely glanced at the sign and, using the railing, climbed the stairs. On the mezzanine floor, he moved as if he had been there many times before and knew the place well.

At Bolivar's door, he paused and listened. When he was sure the office was empty, he went to work on the lock. Thirty seconds later he was inside with the door locked behind him.

The office was a single room, and a mess. There was a

blackboard with chalk and erasers, and there seemed to be papers everywhere.

Shedding his coat in the heat, Carter laid it across the smaller of the two desks, and pulled on a pair of surgical gloves. Then he went to work.

He went through file cabinets, storage closets, and both desks without disturbing the organized chaos of a single piece of paper. He even checked the pens and old-fashioned inkwells on the desks.

Nothing, other than discovering that Domingo Bolivar had a very profitable business and, from his correspondence, a very wide range of friends in several countries.

Next was the bathroom. Other than needing a good scouring, it also yielded nothing. The walls, floors, blinds, and drapes were equally clean.

A safe, scarcely concealed by a Goya print, was so easy to open that Carter hardly had to go through it to discover nothing.

One thing did catch his eye: a first-class air ticket to Rio for the following Monday morning.

Making a mental note of the time and flight number, he relocked the safe and checked the office. When he was positive that everything was in the same place, he eased himself through the door and locked it behind him.

He checked his watch: 4:55.

On the street, he tapped his way two doors down to an outdoor cafe. Taking one of the corner tables facing the street, he ordered a beer and waited.

At precisely five o'clock, Domingo Bolivar walked out of the building across the street. Carter checked the photo in his palm against the man.

He was a pleasant-looking man in a lightweight tan business suit. His hair was sparse and completely gray, and he looked to be about six feet tall. As he crossed the street, he was stooped and walked with a slight limp.

The Killmaster waited until Bolivar was out of sight for five minutes, and then he located the café's pay phone. Dolores Martinez picked up on the first ring.

"It's me. Anything?"

"Crifasi checked in. Nothing."

"Okay. His office is clean. You were right. There is nothing there that would connect him to a damn thing. He's a cautious man. Give me a rundown on the Tarifa villa."

"Let me get my notes."

Carter let his eye wander. Siesta was over and the café was filling up. Two young girls in brightly colored dresses giggled near his booth. Two tables from them, an old woman kept fingering a coin as if she wanted to use the phone. At a table by the street, an enormous man with a nearly bald, bullet head sat sipping a beer. Just as the man looked directly at him, Carter turned away.

"I'm back."

"Yeah."

Dolores Martinez described the villa and the devious route to get to it. "He has a cleaning woman twice a week, Tuesday and Saturday."

"Is she as punctual as he?"

"As near as I have been able to find out, yes," she replied.

"Okay, but I don't think it would be wise for a blind man to drive up there in the middle of the day. Put your phone on the machine and pick me up. I'll be walking north on Calle de Sesto."

"Ten minutes," she replied, and hung up.

The old woman darted for the booth the instant Carter vacated it. He returned to his table and his beer.

Out of the corner of the dark wraparound, he noticed the big man frowning in his direction. The man's brutish head rested directly on his shoulders. He had practically no neck, and his tiny, watery eyes were embedded in fat, puffy hollows.

Carter also noticed that his lightweight white suit was soaked with perspiration.

The Killmaster dropped some pesetas on the table and stood. So did the brute, and moved his way.

"*Perdóneme, señor . . .*"

"*Sí?*" Carter replied.

"Señor, I see that you are blind, so I just wanted to tell you . . ."

"*Sí?*"

"The back of your coat, señor . . . you must have spilled ink on it or something. I just thought I would tell you."

Carter made a show of being flustered. "*Gracias, señor.* Thank you. These things happen."

"Of course."

"*Muchas gracias,*" Carter said, and moved down the street.

Damn, he thought. It was a wonder the whole suit wasn't stained. He had probably laid the coat right across one of the many spills from the inkwells.

Behind him, the big man watched from the shade of the canopy. When Carter crawled into a white Mercedes, he noted the license number, and strolled to the pay phone recently vacated by the old woman.

The routine of the beach umbrella, the chair, and the Spanish beer was the same. When she returned to crouch beside him and pour the beer, Zapato spoke.

"What time do you get out of here?"

"It's Friday night, so everyone will probably leave the beach early to dress for parties and the casino. I'd say we should be locked up by nine."

"Good. The car is parked across the street. Here are the keys."

124

"You want me to pick you up?"

"Yes, at ten sharp, in the casino parking lot. I'll be gambling until then. I want to make sure their plans don't change and they get on that yacht."

"I'll be there," Lucie said, and moved away.

Carter relocked the veranda doors and dropped to the beach. He jogged in the sand for a hundred yards and climbed the rocks until he reached the cutout where Dolores Martinez waited.

Still panting, he slid into the front seat and mopped his face with a handkerchief.

"Well?"

"Nothing," he sighed, "not a damn thing. The house is so clean it's ridiculous. The guy can't keep everything in his head. He must have to write *something* down."

"You searched everywhere?"

"Honey, not to brag, but I'm an expert. I even sent a pipe cleaner down his tube of toothpaste. What does he do on Friday nights and weekends?"

"Let's see," she said, consulting a notebook. "On Friday nights he takes his sister to dinner. They usually go out for a few drinks after that. Saturdays and Sundays, it's the beach below his villa. That's it."

"Christ," Carter groaned. "If this guy wasn't in import-export, he'd be a priest. Something isn't fitting here."

Dolores shrugged. "What now?"

"Back to your place and some sleep and food. I'll pick him up at his office at nine o'clock."

TWELVE

Carter was slouched in the front seat of the battered Peugeot. He was dressed in a dark, summerweight suit. It was nine-thirty, and he was parked in an alley a block from 14 Calle de Sesto. He could see the entrance and he could see the light still burning in the mezzanine office of Domingo Bolivar.

He had been in the alley since eight-thirty. No one had gone in or gone out in that time.

Bolivar was working late. This, coupled with the ticket to Rio, was making Carter very nervous. If the man thought he was blown, he might decide to run that night.

Then the light went out and Carter was instantly alert. Minutes later, two men appeared on the street. One was Bolivar. The other was a short, stocky man with a mane of black hair and a mustache. They both carried briefcases and seemed to be in high spirits.

They laughed, shook hands, and the shorter man walked away. Bolivar crossed the street and got into his car, a late-model white Simca.

Carter cranked up the Peugeot, and when the white car pulled out he slid in behind it.

All he could hope for now, he thought, following the car through traffic, was that there could be some connection through the sister.

Could Bolivar's sister, Marguerita, be the Black Bear?

She lived in Marbella. Sure enough, Bolivar was keeping to his routine. He took the coast highway at the harbor, and headed north toward the resort city. Carter let two cars slide in between them and stayed with him.

Bolivar seemed to be in no hurry, and not once did he do a check for a tail or try to evade. The man, Carter decided, was absolutely sure of himself, or else he just didn't care.

Just short of Marbella, the Simca took a left and started climbing into the hills. Carter had the sister's address, so he hung back.

No problem. By the time the Killmaster had the Simca in sight again, it was parked in front of a new, five-story apartment house. Bolivar was still in the car.

Carter parked in a nearby apartment complex and watched. Five minutes passed, and a woman emerged.

She was a handsome woman, about fifty, tall, with graying black hair and long legs under a knee-length skirt. Her clothes looked expensive and she carried herself with authority. She fit Marguerita Bolivar's description.

Bolivar moved around the car, embraced the woman, kissed both cheeks, and handed her into the Simca.

Carter gave him a three-block head start and then headed out. A mile and a half on up into the hills, they stopped at a small bar. The Killmaster parked across the street and watched.

A cigarette later they were out again and moving. For about twenty minutes they drove parallel to the ocean. Far to his right, Carter could see the ugly high-rises of Torremolinos blocking the view of the ocean.

He had already guessed their destination as the small, whitewashed village of Mijas, and he was right. Minutes later they pulled into La Boveda del Flamenco's parking lot. By the time they were at the door, Carter had already slipped into a space and was heading their way across the street.

It was risky, very risky, but Carter had to take the chance. He wanted to know every move Bolivar made.

In the foyer, he took a quick survey of the configuration. It was perfect. Two dining rooms, with a dark bar to the side. Bolivar and sister were just being seated in the far dining room.

"*Buenos noches, señor*. Will you be dining?"

"No," Carter replied, "drinking. I'll just sit at the bar."

The place was crowded, but he managed to get a stool where he could practically read the couple's lips and they would have a hard time spotting him.

"Señor?"

"Sangria," Carter told the barman. "A pitcher."

The man gave him an odd look, but moved away to fill the order. A pitcher of sangria would be better than nursing drinks. Carter somehow felt it was going to be a long dinner.

Felipe Zapato sat at a roulette table near a window and across the room from the countess's party. It was nearly ten-thirty, and he had begun to think that they would never leave.

Twice he had seen the uniformed steward from the launch whisper in the countess's ear, only to be waved away. Out the window he could see the launch below, and in the middle of the harbor, the Greek's huge yacht.

At last the countess stood and started from the room. Zapato sighed with relief as the others rose and followed. He followed them with his eyes to the launch, and watched its bow lift as it streaked for the yacht.

"Double zero, monsieur. You have won."

Without looking down at the table, Zapato waved his hand at the croupier to let it ride. He was more interested in the launch. Every second was agonizing as he watched the launch being hoisted aboard.

"Double zero again . . . monsieur . . ."

Again Zapato waved his hand. His eyes burned as he concentrated on the stern of the yacht. Then he saw it. The twin screws began to turn, and behind the yacht he could see a frothy white wake.

The night's cruise had begun.

"Fourteen . . . red."

Zapato sighed with relief and pushed himself from his chair. Idly, he glanced at double zero, and his stomach twisted. He counted as the croupier raked the chips from the number he had let ride twice.

Damn, he thought, with less than two thousand francs in his pocket he had just won—and lost—thirty thousand.

Carter was getting a little bleary from the sangria and lack of food. Bolivar and sister were on their third course and hadn't even left the table.

"More sangria, señor?"

"Uh . . . no. Could I get a sandwich here at the bar?"

"Sandwich?"

"Yeah, any kind of sandwich."

The barman shrugged, shook his head, and moved away. Carter returned his concentration to Bolivar's fast-moving lips. As far as the Killmaster could tell, the man was telling his sister that in the morning they would put flowers on their mother's grave.

Christ, Carter thought, *I'm slipping a cog someplace.*

* * *

"You're late," Lucie said, starting the car as Zapato rolled into the rear seat.

"Couldn't be helped. They kept gambling. Move!"

She drove steadily up into the hills, keeping to the speed limit. By the time she had reached the cutout above the villa, he had shed the old man's clothing and sat beside her all in black.

"You know the routine."

"I do. Good luck."

Zapato was already out of the car and moving down the hill. It was a replay of the previous night. Somewhere in the distance, a dog barked a few times. There was no other sound but the rush of the wind through the scrub and the tinny creak of the streetlight on its pole, no movement but the dancing shadows; no clouds scudded between the earth and the sliver of a moon.

Zapato went down the rope ladder like a cat and around the pool. In seconds he was crouching by the lead wires that led through the wall to the alarm system.

The system was controlled by small rectangular sensors that hung from the ceiling in every room of the house. They were very sophisticated sound detectors that could pick up sound or movement within a twenty-yard radius, even through walls. Their control was the computer in the wine cellar that recorded impulses and passed or caused an alarm to go off by what it heard.

From his previous night's inspection from the roof, Zapato already knew that the system was composed of a series of physical-intrusion detection devices. There were vibration strips on the windows, microswitches on the doors, and a layered system of interlocking pressure devices, probably on sections of the flooring in key rooms. All of these would be controlled by the central computer system in the wine cellar.

By the time he had peeled apart the outer layer of the conduit and separated the wiring, Zapato's face and torso were bathed in perspiration.

One mistake there and the evening was over. All he could do was run, and run fast.

Carefully, he separated the wires and, one by one, by-passed them to a tiny voltmeter by his side. It was a simple device, the kind that controlled the current to model trains as they were switched from track to track.

When he was sure that each wire had been covered, and that no matter what impulse they received from the sensors in the villa, they would relay steady electronic impulses to the computer, he ran along the high wall of the villa until he reached the lower servants' wing.

If he had erred in his computations, this was the quickest way back out, since the servants' quarters themselves were probably not wired.

It was high and narrow, a slit in the thick outer wall of the villa overlooking the gardens. He had to squeeze to get through the upper ledge without exposing himself against the night sky.

He was halfway through when he heard the single honk of a horn in the distance. Somewhere in the villa a light had gone on and Lucie had seen it. Hopefully it was the old cook going to the bathroom, but in any event Zapato didn't dare move.

He sat that way, in limbo between the two ledges, for five minutes, until the girl sent the all-clear with three quick honks of the horn.

When the all-clear came, Zapato leaned forward until he was looking down into the interior courtyard that fed into the servants' quarters.

There were no lights below him. He listened for voices, watched for the gleam of a lighted cigarette in the dark, heard nothing, saw nothing.

132

Stretching to his full length from the ledge, he reached around the corner and explored the wall with his fingers until he found a crevice between the stones.

When he did, he began to slither down, a gray shadow against gray rock.

He was known as the Fabulous Greek for good reason. His yacht parties along the Côte d'Azur were legendary. And well they should be. The yacht, the *Delphi,* was a fifteen-million-dollar oceangoing palace with a permanent crew of fifty.

Aside from the crew there were four chefs—one French, one Greek, one Hungarian, one Viennese—sixteen security guards, a resident physican, a resident accountant, a resident dietician, a resident masseur and a resident masseuse (who had three beautiful assistant resident masseuses), two pilots for the seaplane on the top deck, two switchboard operators to control seventy-one telephones connected by radio to the landlocked outside world, and twenty maintenance people to care for the mosaic-tiled dance floor of the ballroom, the swimming pool, the baths with their solid-gold fixtures and marble tubs, and the commodious staterooms.

The Fabulous Greek knew no boundaries in business. He dealt the world over, so the guests on his yacht hailed from both East and West. For this reason, intrigue was rampant. It was a great place for the countess to glean and exchange information, as well as to renew old contacts. Members of the other side, of course, were doing the same thing.

They were about an hour out of port when the countess got her revelation from a Madrid businessman who, when he wasn't feeding information to the West, brokered arms for the Russians in Africa. The moment the countess got her information, she caught Natalia Mydova's eye and headed for the lower decks.

When they both had checked the powder room just off the

133

main salon, they slipped into adjoining stalls with pens in hand and pads on knees. Soon, scribbled notes were being passed under the partitions:

Countess to Mydova: *Contact says intelligence coup of the century coming down this Sunday. Major Western ring could be exposed. All contact's friends have been alerted to move.*

Mydova to countess: *Fits. I have been instructed to attend bullfights in Madrid week from Sunday. Am to pick up microfilm then and carry to Rome.*

Countess to Mydova: *What then?*

Mydova to countess: *Return with orders for Stringent to Madrid and on to Paris.*

The countess read the last note and felt her whole body break out in a cold sweat. *Stringent* was the KGB code for blanket arrests and/or assassinations. Whatever they thought they had uncovered had far-reaching ramifications.

Countess to Mydova: *Do as you are told. Will make arrangements for possible intercept in Madrid. Meantime I must get back to villa and notify my people.*

Without waiting for an answer, the countess vacated the powder room and hurried to find the Fabulous Greek. She had already formulated ten fraudelent excuses in her mind as to why she had to get back to the mainland at once.

And back in the powder room, in her stall, Natalia Mydova was going through the same cold sweat.

Intelligence coup of the century . . . . Major Western ring . . . exposed . . . .

Could it be, the ballerina wondered, the same ring of which she was such an integral part?

THIRTEEN

The old cook looked tiny as she slept bathed in moonlight in the immense bed. Mouth half open, she trailed a hand across the thin coverlet in drugged sleep.

Zapato, a pencil flash in his teeth, moved across the room and gently opened the door. It creaked a little when it opened, and he tensed. He pulled his eyes back to the woman. She had not moved. Breathing a silent sigh of relief, he closed the door on the sleeping woman and slipped silently to the head of the stairs.

Down below, light filtered into the wide hall that led to the study. The two mortise locks on the door were secured, the keys gone. Zapato tried skeleton keys, failed, and resorted to picks.

It took all of five minutes before the locks gave and the heavy door opened on well-oiled hinges.

Four minutes later, the outer safe was open. The combination from the television remote control was the same, but the inner liner was a different make. It took Zapato a few seconds to decipher that it was a direct pull-out.

This done, and the liner on the floor, he went to work on the second safe. It was much newer and far more advanced than the model in the Seville house. For a full fifteen minutes he worked before he had to step back, relax the tension in his body, and wipe the perspiration from his eyes.

He checked his watch. He had been in the villa for twenty-two minutes. He was eight minutes behind schedule.

A tall grandfather clock in the corner whirred the half hour as he attacked the safe again.

This time he was calmer. His fingers achieved the artistry he knew they possessed. One by one, through the stethoscope in his ears, he heard the tumblers fall into place. Twice he had all but one number in the combination, went too far, and had to start over.

At last he heard the final click and pulled the door open. Still holding the light in his teeth, he looked inside.

They were there, both books, and a bonus: a diamond and platinum watch, a ruby necklace with matching earrings, and a cloverleaf diamond ring. This time the gems were real.

Zapato shoved everything into a specially sewn pouch in the turtleneck and replaced the safe. After a quick check of the room, he moved back into the hall. He was halfway across the house to the servants' quarters, when, in the distance, he heard a single blast from a horn. A split second later the front windows were bathed with light.

Zapato ducked, his whole body quivering.

Impossible, he thought. *They've returned, they are back. But they can't be. They are miles out to sea.*

But as he watched the headlights move around the villa toward the garage area, his hopes dimmed. They dimmed even further when the engine died and he heard the countess's voice barking orders at her chauffeur.

To make matters worse, a light came on in the old cook's room. That way of escape was out.

Zapato heard the door between the kitchen and the garage open, and sprinted across to the opposite stairs.

On flying feet he worked his way up through the villa from the bottom floor, peering through outside windows and trying doors.

Most of the guest room doors he found securely locked, and with the voices getting louder from below he had no time to pick any of them.

He would need a window, to the outside, to the roof.

After climbing interminable flights of stairs, he found one, opened it, and dropped to one of the rear roofs. From there it would be an easy descent via drainpipe.

He was about to roll over the edge, when the whole pool area lit up. At the same time, the countess appeared on the patio.

"I am going to change. Make some coffee, lots of it, and bring two phones out here where it's cool. It's going to be a long night."

She disappeared, but two men and the old cook bustled between the great room, the kitchen, and the patio. Twice, while bringing a table and chairs from the other side of the pool, one of the men came within two feet of the rope ladder.

Zapato hunkered down beside a chimney and forced his mind into high gear. Exiting the same way he had come in was now out of the question.

He checked his watch. In ten minutes, Lucie would pull out of the cutout and wind her way down to the lower road and the cul-de-sac below the villa.

There was only one thing Zapato figured he could do: he would have to go over the front of the villa and work his way through the trees to the front outer wall.

The countess's voice barking orders from an open window not twenty yards from where Zapato crouched confirmed his only option.

He studied the roofs he still had to cross, marking a path that would not take him in front of a dormer window. He had to pass the length of the wing and over the main, higher rooftops to the tower, that rose from the juncture of the opposite wing with the central mass of the villa.

The roofs were of slate tile, smooth and steep. Slate was always dangerous to climb, not only because of its smoothness but because each tile was hung on a single nail that pulled loose easily under strain and might let the tile slide with a revealing clatter. And although there were no dormers overlooking the roof in either wing, several broke the top outline of the main building, one or two showing lighted windows.

He crossed above the dormers, making his way along the gutter to the inner end of the wing, up the angle the roof made with the joining wall, jumping from the peak of the wing to catch the gutter at the eave of the higher roof, then up the rise of the roof corner to the top.

Only the tower stood higher. The central roof was a series of disconnected gables and sharply peaked turrets, so that his path along the ridges of the rooftop, balanced as delicately as a wire walker to avoid a misstep on the sheer slopes of slate, took him up, down, and at angles until he reached the base of the tower.

The eaves and the bulk of the villa itself had shielded him until then from view of anyone who might look up from the garden. The tower was more exposed. He knew there was a stairway inside, and a door opened at the tower base onto a lower roof. But he didn't try the door. He made his way around the tower on the narrow walk to the outer side, where it was blocked by the thick growth of ivy climbing from the ground below.

But he didn't want the ground. He wanted the stout limb of a tree twenty feet away and thirty feet below where he stood.

Casting aside the penlight, Zapato opened his knife and

put it in his teeth. Like a cat he moved back over the roof, around the corner, and started down the ivy. He selected a vine about wrist-thick and cut it away, and he went down. When he was about thirty feet, he cut the vine free.

Twice he kicked out from the wall to make sure the vine was sturdy enough for his weight. When he was satisfied, he started to swing in long arcs around the corner.

It took four tries before he figured he had the momentum. Then he took a deep breath, let go, and sailed . . . .

His fingers slid off the first limb, but he managed to wrap his legs around another and arrest his fall. Without breaking his momentum, he rolled on over and started going from limb to limb and tree to tree.

A squirrel would have been envious of his progress.

In minutes he vaulted over the outer wall and hit the ground running. A hundred yards through the trees he could see the cul-de-sac . . . and the car.

"Lucie!" he called so she wouldn't be alarmed.

She wasn't. She was good. His hand was barely on the door handle when the engine kicked to life. His butt was scarcely in the seat when the car lurched forward.

"How did we do, *chéri?*"

He glanced up from pulling a black bag from the bedroll on the floorboard. Lucie's words were odd and so was her tone. Her eyes were wide and alive, and her lips were curved in a mischievous grin.

"We did fine, *chérie.*"

Zapato put the jewelry in the bag, pulled it taut, and dropped it in her lap. "Can you get that to Ferare?"

"I'll be on the first plane in the morning. You?"

"The rest of the business," he replied, lighting a cigarette and satisfied at how steady his fingers were. "Ferare will give you a nice cut of those."

"I'm not worried," Lucie said, pulling into a parking

space and killing the lights. "If I go to Ferare in Madrid
. . . will I see you?"

"Do you want to see me?"

"I do," she replied, and emphasized it by leaning across
the car and kissing him soundly on the lips.

Zapato was about to slip his arms around her and return
the kiss, when suddenly she was out of the car and darting
toward her apartment house.

"Well, I'll be damned," Zapato chuckled, and restarted
the car.

He drove carefully, keeping just above the speed limit
all the way to Cagnes. After parking behind the motorcycle
shop, he waited a full five minutes in the darkness.

Safe. Quiet.

Taking his time, he wiped the interior of the car and the
exterior handles clean of prints. Then, jimmying the door,
he entered the shop carrying the bedroll.

It took only another five minutes to attach the stolen plate
to a new BMW and tie the bedroll behind the saddle. Then
he rolled the machine out and coasted nearly a mile down
the hill before releasing the clutch and letting the machine
roar to life.

He hit the A4 motorway with the powerful BMW wide
open, and watched the towns fly by.

An hour and a half later, he flew through Aix-en-Provence
and bypassed Marseille. He took the N568 to Arles, and
cut south again to Montpellier where he stole some gas from
a small farmhouse. From there he rode to Béziers where
dawn and his stomach suggested breakfast.

By ten he was at the foot of the Pyrenees directly north
of Andorra, in the tiny village of Vicdessos.

Just south of the village there was a campground. It was
crowded with young people who had come to take the long
hike up the Pyrenees. But they would be hiking by day,

and only to the top of the first big peak.

That night Zapato would ride, by back-mountain trails, all the way over the mountains and down into the valleys of Andorra.

Zapato rented a small cabin and carried his bedroll inside.

His mind and his body craved sleep, but there was still too much work ahead. He would sleep come dawn tomorrow in one of the old shepherds' huts in the mountains around El Serrat.

He took the countess's two leather-covered notebooks from his bedroll, along with two blank notebooks of a similar design.

Carefully, he lined up several ball-point pens and went to work.

By dusk he had copied—at least in style and type of content—the contents of the two stolen books into the two blank ones.

Of course names, references, telephone numbers, and personal descriptions had been totally altered.

Felipe Zapato had been a thief too long to trust anyone.

FOURTEEN

Carter was like a fused stick of dynamite ready to go off. Bolivar had not once acted like a man who was settling up his affairs to skip.

After a two-hour meal, he and his sister had adjourned to another room and watched a half-hour set of flamenco entertainment. When they left at last, Carter was right behind them. There were two stops for after-dinner drinks as they wound their way back to Marbella and the sister's house.

There, the woman got out and Bolivar drove away with Carter again right behind him.

It was easy to keep the taillights in sight. As before, Bolivar was in no hurry. For a moment, climbing and twisting along the narrow mountain road, Carter had hopes that, at last, the man was heading for some kind of contact.

No such luck.

Suddenly they pulled out of a switchback, and Carter could see the whole sweep of the Costa del Sol and the Simca turning south again toward Algeciras. From there it was a boring drive through the city and on to Tarifa.

Carter waited on another road above the villa until the lights went out. It was three-thirty in the morning, and the Killmaster had no more on the man now than he had in the beginning.

In disgust, he turned the Peugeot around and headed back to Algeciras and Dolores Martinez's house. To himself he vowed that if he had nothing concrete by Sunday night, he would move on the man anyhow.

He parked in the garage and walked through the laundry room. Before he reached the inner door he heard her heels beating a quick tattoo on the parquet.

The door was yanked open, and even in the dim light, he could read trouble on her face.

"What is it?"

"I just talked to Crifasi a few moments ago. Bolivar called."

"What?" Carter almost shouted, immediately racking his brain. The man had not been out of his sight once all night, other than two trips to the men's room, and Carter had made sure he hadn't met anyone there nor made a call. "That's impossible!"

"Not according to Madrid. He called Lucchi about two hours ago."

Carter thought hard. Two hours before, they had either been in one of the after-dinner watering holes, or in transit between them. And Bolivar didn't have a telephone in his car.

Carter dived for the phone. "Dig me up a beer."

By the time Joe Crifasi's voice came on the line in Madrid, Carter was pacing the room with the phone in one hand and a second beer in the other.

"Sorry I took so long, Nick. We were double-checking our trace."

"Good," the Killmaster replied, "because that was going to be my first question. You're sure Bolivar called through the Calle de Sesto relay phone?"

"No doubt about it. Bolivar called Tony Lucchi at one twenty-two this morning. Listen up, here's the tape."

There was a few seconds' silence, then a click and the sound of a phone buzz.

"Yes?"

"Tony, this is Bolivar. We have business."

"Yes."

"The man from Naples is here. I think it best you call me back."

"Five minutes," Lucchi replied, and the phone went dead.

Carter's stomach sank to his knees. If that was all the conversation they had, he would learn nothing. And it was ten to one that Tony Lucchi was headed for a neutral pay phone.

He said as much to Crifasi when the other man came back on the line.

"Calm down, Nick. We had that covered from the first day we came aboard. There are five street phones in the immediate area of Lucchi's apartment. My boys bugged them all."

Carter sighed aloud. "Sorry, Joe. Go on."

"The minute Lucchi left the apartment, we had two cars and three pedestrians all over his ass. When we got a line on which phone he was headed for, we made the cut-in."

"Did he dial the relay phone here in Algreciras?" Carter asked.

"No doubt about it. That's why I just got through double-checking. Here's the tape."

Again the same sounds on the line, and the phone in Algeciras was picked up.

"Yes?"

"I'm in the booth," Lucchi's voice said. "Go ahead."

"Fly to Barcelona in the morning. Pick up a car there and drive up to the Roc. Do you understand?"

"Yes."

"Check in, and be on the lookout for a mark. His name, if he is dumb enough to use it, is Felipe Zapato."

"One of ours?"

"No, he's a common thief. He's lifting some very important documents, which I will trade for Sunday night. Try to spot him early if you can. He's about six feet, dark, black hair, handsome man. I'd say around two hundred pounds and very muscular. Has to be—he spends a lot of time on roofs and in trees in his line of work." Here Bolivar paused with a low chuckle.

"You just want me to spot him until you get here?"

"Yes. Don't touch him. I'll be in Sunday about noon and give you the particulars then."

"After you get your goods," Lucchi asked, "do we go wet?"

"Yes. The material is very sensitive. I wouldn't want Zapato to leak its whereabouts back to the real owners."

"Sunday, then."

"Sunday it is," Bolivar replied. "Also, I'll be passing the material the following Sunday in Madrid, at the Plaza de Toros. It might be a good idea if you accompany me as a backup."

"Whatever your bankbook allows, señor. Till Sunday."

The connection was broken and Joe Crifasi came back on the line.

"That's it, Nick. Lucchi went back to his apartment and hit the sack. But, get this, not before he calls Iberia Airlines and makes a reservation for the morning flight to Barcelona. Talk about security!"

Carter was deep in thought, so much so that he didn't speak for a full two minutes.

"Hey, Nick, you still there?"

"Yeah," the Killmaster growled, "I'm still here. Listen, Joe, our main beef in this is the Black Bear first and Lucchi

146

second. That's what we're here for, right?"

"I got you."

"Whatever goods they're picking up might be worth something, or routine."

"I think I'm following you," Crifasi replied.

"Stay on Lucchi like glue. Keep him on ice for me. Bolivar has a Monday ticket to Rio in his safe, and now he's talking about meeting Lucchi at some rock out of Barcelona. I don't want to take a chance on missing him. I'm going for Bolivar tonight."

"We'll be on Lucchi like flies on a corpse. See you."

Carter hung up and sat back with a sigh. Dolores Martinez sat across the room, boring into him with her eyes.

"Do you think that's wise? We haven't got a shred of proof that Bolivar is the Black Bear."

"I know," Carter replied. "And we'll have less than that, I think, if we wait. But I've got a hunch. Let's move. I'll need your help."

She shrugged and stood. "You're the boss. Let me change into some slacks."

"Do that," Carter said, "and bring me back a pair of your panty hose and some scissors."

Dolores scooted from the room. Carter crossed to the sideboard and poured a shot of Chivas.

As the soothing liquid rolled down his throat, he closed his eyes in concentration.

If he was sure of only one thing in this mess, it was that the Domingo Bolivar he was tailing that night was not the Domingo Bolivar that called Tony Lucchi.

They saw only one car on the narrow road leading up to Bolivar's villa: a dusty black Citroen with a buggy-whip radio aerial mounted on one rear fender.

Carter slowed and let it pass. As it did, he sensed Dolores tense in the seat beside him.

"What is it?"

"Police . . . the Citroen."

"Guardia?"

"No, harbor police—customs."

Carter eased back even more on the throttle. The red taillights of the Citroen wound on up the mountain and out of sight.

A mile past the villa, he cut down a narrow dirt road that led to a public parking lot above the beach. He killed the engine and lights on the Mercedes.

"C'mon," he said, crawling from the car and locking it behind him.

"I don't get it," Dolores said, falling in step beside him. "You want me to come in with you? Why?"

"Two reasons. One, I don't want him having a heart attack when I stick this Luger up his left nostril. A woman may have a bit of calming influence. Two, he took a well-stuffed briefcase home with him. If I have to search for it, I want you keeping your eye on him while I do."

By this time they were climbing the steps from the beach to the house. A gate in the wooden fence was locked, but this posed no obstacle. Seconds later they were moving around the pool toward the veranda. Once there, Carter dropped into a crouch and pulled Dolores down beside him.

The house was quiet, no lights. He knew the layout and the easy entry from his first visit.

Using hand motions, he directed Dolores to follow, and made his way up some outside stone stairs to a veranda. At the top, he came to an abrupt halt.

Already he didn't like what he was finding out. Thirty feet in front of them across the terrace were two French doors leading into Domingo Bolivar's bedroom. The French doors were wide open, and beyond them, sleeping like a baby on the bed, was Bolivar.

148

If this man was the Black Bear, Carter thought, nothing up to this moment would point to him.

A quick look at Dolores's startled expression and the Killmaster knew she was thinking along the same lines.

Quietly, he cut the legs out of the panty hose, handed her one, and pulled the other one over his head and face. When she had done the same, they moved into the bedroom.

"Señor Bolivar . . . Señor Domingo Bolivar . . ."

The man grunted half awake and opened his eyes to slits. When he saw the Luger, the eyes came wide and he lurched to an upright position on the bed.

"Mother of God, oh, Holy Mother of God . . . take anything, everything, take all I have . . . there is a safe in the living room . . . take what you find . . ."

"Relax, señor . . ."

"I have no cash here, I'll write you a check . . . Mother of God, just don't shoot me!"

Carter exchanged a look with Dolores Martinez. They were obviously both thinking the same thing.

Domingo Bolivar wasn't their target.

"Calm down, Señor Bolivar," Carter said, passing a glass of brandy from Dolores to him. "We are not going to rob you."

"Then why . . . ?"

Carter put the gun away. "We are looking for a man, and we think that somehow you might be able to help us."

Alexander Czarkis sat in the cluttered office of Domingo Bolivar and sipped ice water in an attempt to allay the heat that constantly pestered his body.

He had been sitting like this, in the darkness, for hours, since he had called Lucchi in Madrid and taken the return call.

Earlier than that, the two federal customs agents who had

been on his private payroll for over two years had called to tell him that they had located the Mercedes.

"Watch it, but don't move on it unless the man is in it," he had told them. "Then call me back."

Now Czarkis was sweating. He knew Nick Carter was on to Lucchi in Italy. Had he traced the dapper little killer to Spain? It wouldn't appear so. Lucchi had told him he was sure he was clean.

But Czarkis was positive that the blind man in the café had been Carter, and from the Moscow report that meant that he, Czarkis, was in trouble if the American agent was in Algeciras.

The red light on the phone's intercom button, the one that never came on when the real Bolivar was in the office, was lit.

Czarkis grabbed the instrument with one huge, sweaty paw. "*Sí?*"

"Señor Bolivar?"

"This is he."

"The man returned to the woman's house. Soon they both left in the Mercedes. It is strange, señor . . ."

"Strange? What do you mean?"

"We followed them to your villa, señor. They parked near the beach and entered your house. They are there now."

Czarkis felt a pain in his belly. It was the ulcer he had developed after eating ten years of the terrible food in this stinking country. Also, another pint of perspiration poured from him as he forced his mind to a decision.

"You will go ahead," he said at last.

"The woman, too, señor?"

"Of course the woman too!" Czarkis barked. "It won't be the first woman you have killed for me!"

"No, señor."

"Like the others, lose their bodies at sea. Payment will

be made in the usual way. And, as always, don't approach me in person. And don't approach them until they are a safe distance from my villa. Do you understand this?"

"Of course, Señor Bolivar, it will be done as you ask."

Czarkis returned the phone to its cradle and folded his hands over his huge paunch.

The woman was probably a local agent. He was surprised he didn't know of her existence. But then he, the Black Bear, had operated in Spain for ten years and no one knew of *him*.

So Nick Carter was at Bolivar's villa. He was probably interrogating the old fool. Of course he would learn nothing, but if Carter was as good as Moscow's report claimed he was, he would probably be putting the puzzle together.

Even if Carter and the woman didn't survive the night, it was ridiculous to take chances. The American agent might have passed on a report of his suspicions. When he and the woman disappeared, someone else would come looking.

Czarkis heaved his huge body from the chair and, leaving the door to Bolivar's office open, climbed the stairs to his own office.

The Black Bear had had a long—and very successful—ten-year run. It was time for Czarkis to return to his native Prague and reap the rewards of so many years of service. And with the coup he would pass on in Madrid, the rewards from Moscow would be more than enough for his retirement.

He had already planned for an emergency earlier in the evening. All the most important papers, the ciphers, and the code book were in a briefcase on his desk. He draped the long strap of the briefcase around his neck and over his shoulder, and lifted the two five-gallon cans of gasoline.

Liberally, he soaked his office and the small apartment, and made a wide trail of the liquid down the stairs. When the first can went dry he discarded it and shifted to the full one. By the time the second can was empty, Bolivar's office was also soaked with gas and the trail ran down to the lobby.

After unlocking the front door, he turned, folded back a book of matches, and lit them. When the matches hit the gas, it moved up the stairs like an angry, fiery snake.

By the time the two offices had burst into flames, Czarkis was in his car headed for the small private airfield near Marbella.

FIFTEEN

Carter checked the silk ties that bound Domingo Bolivar one last time and motioned Dolores to follow him.

"The cleaning woman will find him in a few hours. In the meantime, he won't be making any phone calls."

Together they hit the beach and sprinted toward the car. Halfway there, Dolores was full of questions. "You really think it's this Czarkis?"

"I don't doubt it for a minute. He's been Bolivar's accountant for eight years. He keeps a low profile, has no friends, even lives beside his office. He's had the run of Bolivar's office for five years, comes and goes as he pleases with his own keys. You heard Bolivar. Czarkis often works on his books in the morning before Bolivar arrives, and sometimes in the evenings after he leaves."

"It would figure," she panted. "By using Bolivar's name and office, Czarkis would be forewarned if anybody came after the real Bolivar. Slick."

"Very," Carter said with a nod, yanking the door open and crawling in. "Let's just hope he doesn't know about you and hasn't spotted me."

He came out of the parking lot in a swirl of gravel and

hurtled down the narrow hillside road toward the corniche. The moment he hit the approach ramp, he floored the Mercedes.

He had barely gone a mile when a pair of headlights appeared behind them coming fast, much faster than anything he could get out of the Mercedes.

It smelled, especially at this hour of the morning and on this particular stretch of highway.

He glanced in the rearview mirror, and then again. And then a third time. "I think we're being followed," he growled.

Dolores swung her head around. "How can you tell?" she asked after a moment.

"I'm not sure I'm right, not yet. But the set of those headlights is distinctive. I think I've noticed them before." He saw the sign for the turnoff and swung into the right lane. The car behind followed.

Carter grabbed the next cutoff, hit the beach road, and stomped on the brake. The little car screamed a lot, but it performed like a Mercedes should and did a full turn, ending up with its nose back toward the corniche ramp.

Seconds later, the black Citroen with the buggy-whip aerial came off the corniche and headed their way.

"Nick, it's the customs police!"

"Oh, yeah? They're a long way from the docks, but I'll give 'em one chance."

He took the Luger out, fingered the safety off, and placed it between his legs. As he jiggled the foot feed with his right toe, he kept the clutch partly out under his left foot, ready to drop it and make tracks if he had to run.

The Citroen slowed, veered to the right, and came up alongside. They slowed as the black car's rear door came up just opposite Carter.

"Anything wrong?" he called out in Spanish, plastering a smile on his face.

SPYKILLER

There were two mean-looking men in the front seat. The words were scarcely out of Carter's mouth when a third one came up out of the back seat with an automatic in both hands.

"Down!" Carter shouted, and dropped the clutch. The rear wheels screamed and the Mercedes lurched forward. A slug tore through the rear window and Carter shoved his foot to the floor. "Cops, my ass. You all right?"

"Glass in my hair, but I'm okay. But I know that's a customs car."

"Maybe so," Carter hissed, "but if they are cops, they're drawing two payrolls."

Through the shattered rear window he could see that the Citroen had spun around, and from the bouncing light he knew they were going to give chase.

"There's a curve up ahead. I'm going to speed up, cut the headlights, and pull over to the side of the road once we get around it. Hang on!"

He floored the accelerator, roared into the curve, tires barely making contact, then slammed off the lights and wheeled abruptly away from the asphalt, driving straight at the shadow of a tree, then veering off to its side and totally obscuring the Mercedes in the night shadows.

The Citroen, with its aerial whipping in the wind, thundered by and suddenly picked up even more speed, as if anxious to catch up to something.

"Looks as though you were right," Dolores said.

Carter said nothing. He pulled out onto the road, lights off, then headed back in the direction they'd come.

"Do you think we're safe?" Dolores asked.

"No. They'll come back looking for us near that curve as soon as they don't spot our taillights in front of them," Carter answered. "We'll drive a while and stop and see what happens."

Two miles down the highway he went into another U-turn and again pulled to the side of the road. Nothing showed,

and ten minutes later they were once more driving toward
Algeciras.

Three miles went by, and again there were the lights of
a car behind them. They were like those before: close-set
and high.

"You've got to give them credit. They know their job,"
Carter said tightly.

"What now?" Dolores asked.

"We try again," Carter said.

The Mercedes abruptly picked up speed as a curve approached, but this turn was too short, and there was no time
to leave the road.

"They seem to be gaining on us," Dolores said coolly.

"The better for us to see them," Carter muttered as he
pulled the hand brake and swerved to the right.

As he'd expected, the car behind, caught short by the
maneuver, the use of the emergency brake keeping the Mercedes's brake lights from flashing, involuntarily shot past
them.

The Citroen slowed, moving into the wrong lane, waiting
for the Mercedes to catch up.

"We haven't got the horses," Carter hissed. "They can
play games all night. We're gonna have to take 'em."

"My God, Nick, you can't be serious!" Dolores cried.

"Oh, but I am."

He whipped to the left, through a short fence and down
an embankment into a field. The car bounced and groaned
as it hurtled over the uneven ground. Twenty yards short
of a grove of trees, he braked and killed the engine and lights.

"Out, fast! Head for those trees!"

They made the trees and Carter passed the Luger over.
"Can you use this?"

"Of course."

"Good. If they fire, keep 'em busy and distracted. But

don't fire from the same place twice. As soon as you draw their fire, don't wait, move fast!"

The Citroen came crashing down over the embankment and up to the Mercedes. Doors opened and bodies spilled out the instant the lights and engine were killed.

Carter moved out. The field was plowed. He dropped between the furrows and belly-crawled like a crab. The moonlight was an enemy, but there wasn't much of him showing.

Dolores helped by pumping a slug from the Luger into the grill of the Citroen. Immediately, she drew answering fire and Carter made better time.

His hand hit something: a two-by-four piece of wood about three feet long. It must have been a marker stake or something, because it was shaved sharp at one end. It wasn't Wilhelmina, but it was better than nothing.

Twenty feet later, he froze. Footsteps were coming his way. Then he saw the outline of a man, bulky, crouched low. Evidently this one had the same plan of encirclement that Carter was following.

The Killmaster's grip tightened on the two-by-four. A quick strike at the man's gut should put him out of action, knock the wind out of him.

He was close now, sharply etched against the dark as the moon broke through a cloud. With the moon behind Carter, there was no way the gunman could see him. He braced himself.

The man was almost on him, coming in a direct line. Carter went into a crouch and shoved the two-by-four straight at the midsection.

He had misjudged the sharpness of the end of the two-by-four, and the softness of the bulky man's belly. The wood stopped for a moment and then, as the outer flesh parted, continued in, one inch, two inches, until almost a foot of it was embedded. Carter loosened his grasp, and the man, eyes wide, fell backward in a sitting position, his mouth in a small circle, like that of a gaping fish. Little bubbles of blood began to form there, and he continued to sit, astonishment written on his face, oblivious of his assailant, who was now pulling a Beretta out of his hand.

Two shots sounded, evidently from Dolores, and they were answered. Carter took a final look at his victim, whose eyes were beginning to glaze, a thin trickle of blood oozing over his thick lower lip. No need to finish him off; he seemed too deep in shock to warn anyone by screaming out.

Carter hit the ground again and moved in the direction of the gunfire.

He reached about where he thought the gun would be, and stopped. Everything was still.

Another shot, baby, he thought. *Shoot again, so he fires back at you.*

A few more seconds, and Dolores obliged. A few feet away, a man rose and answered the lone bullet with a fusillade.

Carter waited for silence, then shouted, "Throw down the gun!"

"Bastard!" the man hissed, and wheeled on Carter.

The Killmaster pumped two slugs into the center of the man's chest, and dropped with him. He moved forward, only to find the shooter still willing. The mortally wounded man was desperately trying to bring his piece up with both hands for another shot.

Carter pumped a third slug into the center of his forehead, and rolled to the side behind the Citroen.

Another shot came from the grove of trees. Carter recognized the bark of the Luger. This one wasn't returned.

Suddenly, far to his right, came a voice. "Milo? Juan?"

Carter smiled. How long would it be before Number Three realized that Señors Milo and Juan had taken the long sleep and he was now all by his lonesome?

The Killmaster took a sighting from the last sound of the voice, and started to flank that way. Suddenly there was a blur in front of him and a flash of orange.

He felt the slug whistle by his ear, and dived. He heard running feet. Seconds later the engine of the Citroen roared to life.

"Shit," Carter wheezed, and rolled up over the furrow.

He raised his head, straightened out his arm, and took careful aim. The silhouette of the big car was murky in the moonlight, and he hoped he was seeing right. He squeezed the trigger once, twice.

A giant explosion filled the air. His aim had been true, and one of the bullets had hit the vehicle's gas tank, rupturing it and igniting the volatile fuel.

Carter rushed forward, standing out in the moonlight, chancing that he'd succeeded.

A few steps nearer, and in the light of the vehicle's flames, he saw he had. Number Three was ten feet away from the car, his clothes in shreds, face and body blackened, half his side blown away. He was still alive, and when he saw Carter, his hand and arm twitched convulsively, as if searching for the automatic that had been blasted out of his hand. Carter bent down to do what he could, taking a huge clump of sod and stuffing it into the gaping wound. Anything to stop the bleeding.

But it was too late. The face was already skull-like as death rushed into him, gnawing and ravaging. No time for the idiocy of making his last moments comfortable.

"Why?" the Killmaster growled. "Who hired you?"

The man stared up at him, even tried to reach out. But the sound was only a gurgle. He tried again to speak, but it was too much. His body sagged, then collapsed, his head flopping to one side, the eyes staring vacantly.

Carter stood, sighed, and turned at a sound behind him. It was Dolores, still holding the Luger in both hands at the ready position to fire.

"Is he . . . ?"

"Yeah," Carter muttered, "they all are. Let's get back to Algeciras. I've got a hunch we're not going to find a hell of a lot."

Carter was right. They wouldn't find a trace of Alexander Czarkis.

They spotted the smoke on the outskirts of the city, and the flames about eight blocks away. Carter pulled into a parking space about two blocks away, killed the lights, and, with a sigh, lit a cigarette.

Flames were leaping a hundred feet into the air from 14 Calle de Sesto. They counted four fire engines, a half-dozen police cars, and even a Jeep full of Guardia Civil officers.

"You don't suppose," Dolores asked, her tone dripping with sarcasm, "that we would be lucky enough to find his bones in there?"

"No, I don't suppose we would."

"What now?"

"We go back to your place, regroup. You call the contacts around here and see what you can get on this Czarkis . . . background, photo, anything. I'll do the same in Washington. Since the Black Bear has survived this long, I doubt we'll find a damn thing, but we've got to try."

He turned the car around and they drove in silence all the way back to her house.

The red light was blinking on Dolores's answering machine. She reran the tape and let it play:

"Dolores, I'm at the number in Nice. Call me at once." They both recognized the countess's voice.

"Call her back," Carter said. "I'll use the second line from the bedroom phone."

He grabbed the bottle of scotch and a glass from the sideboard, and headed for the bedroom. He had barely dialed half the digits for a Washington call, when he sensed Dolores in the doorway. Her hands were gripping the front of her thighs and her face was chalky. Her dark eyes were like saucers.

"Nick, you'd better take it . . . line two."

He grabbed the instrument and punched the second button. "Yeah, Bea, Nick here."

"We've got trouble, Nick. Big trouble."

Carter chain-smoked, sipped scotch, and listened. Only twice did he interrupt the woman and have her repeat. By the time she finished, ripples were crawling up the Killmaster's back.

"Our only chance," the countess continued, "is that it was a common thief and aside from the jewels he doesn't know what he's got."

"I'm afraid we don't have that chance," came Carter's whispered reply.

There were fifteen full seconds of silence from the other end of the line before she spoke again. "What do you mean by that?"

Tersely, he relayed the night's events and the content, as well as he could remember it, of the telephone conversation between Tony Lucchi in Madrid and the man he now knew as Czarkis.

"Oh, Christ, Nick, we've got to intercept this Zapato!"

"Try to get a line from your end," Carter said. "I'll work from here with Crifasi. In the meantime, keep alerting your people that they might be on the verge of being blown. And one thing more . . ."

"Yes?"

"Natalia Mydova. Have her stay in constant touch with her KGB superiors, and make sure she gets on that flight to Madrid. If we miss, she may be our last chance."

NICK CARTER

He hung up and moved back to the living room with Dolores on his heels.

"I'm calling Joe back. Rig that thing up so it will record."

As soon as the machine was ready, Carter put through the call. This time Joe Crifasi himself answered.

"Have you been able to break anything out of that tape yet?"

"*Nada,* Nick, but there are only three of us here and we don't know the area."

"Okay, play it this way again. I'm going to record at this end."

"Got you. Here it comes."

Carter paced and listened as the recording was made. As soon as it ended, he grabbed the phone. "Joe, me again."

"Yeah."

"Domingo Bolivar was a beard. The real one is named Alexander Czarkis. He's been in Algeciras as an accountant for about ten years. If he isn't the Bear himself, he knows who is. Get everything you can on him."

"Will do."

"I'll get back to you if we come up with anything at this end."

For the next hour, the two of them played and replayed the tape over and over again.

Carter made mental notes and scrawled on a yellow legal pad. There was little doubt in his mind that they had stumbled on a two-for-one. And knowing the ways of thieves and fences, he could extrapolate the series of events to a thief and a Soviet agent.

The countess had said that Joanna Dubshek's cover was deep and foolproof. Yet she had been hit, and hit by Tony Lucchi. From the feel of it, Lucchi worked directly for Czarkis.

It was ten to one that the thief was Felipe Zapato, and

he had offered a sample to Czarkis of the countess's journal to make a deal.

That "sample" had been Joanna Dubshek.

"Anything?" Dolores asked, bringing a fresh pot of coffee from the kitchen.

Carter shook his head. *"Nada.* 'The rock' is probably Gibraltar, but it doesn't figure. Getting on and off Gibraltar is damn hard, for security reasons. It's a lousy place for this kind of a meet and exchange."

She poured the coffee and went back to her own notes. About ten minutes later, she yelped.

"What is it?"

"I don't know . . . maybe. Nick, play the tape through again."

Carter rewound the tape and played it through again. This time he didn't listen. He watched Dolores Martinez's face and saw bells going off in her head.

"I've got it!" she cried. "It's not the Rock—Gibraltar. It's the Roc—R-O-C—the Hotel Roc in Andorra! Czarkis told him to rent a car in Barcelona and drive up to the Roc and check in. That's it, Nick, I'm sure of it!"

Carter kissed her and dived for the telephone.

SIXTEEN

Golden lights above the door spelled out the word DISCO.
The inside of the club had the same glitzy, golden glitter,
the same disco play of lights.

Felipe Zapato, dressed in a dark turtleneck, dark trousers,
and a light blue blazer, entered and took a table in the
shadows far from the dance floor.

The disco was in Port d'Envalira, far enough from the capital of Andorra-la-Vella that he felt it was safe enough to
show himself for a short time.

He had spent the entire day in the hills above Port d'Envalira in an abandoned barn. That was where the BMW was
now. Just after darkness, he had changed clothes and come
down into the village.

What he was up to was a long shot, but if he could pull
it off, there would be a certain amount of safety he wouldn't
have if going in cold.

The disco was crowded when he entered. There were
French tourists from across the frontier, locals, and a few
Spaniards up from Barcelona to escape the heat for a
weekend in the mountains.

Zapato ordered a beer and watched the dancers as well

as everyone coming in and leaving.

It was two hours before he made up his mind.

She was around forty, strong as a horse and resembled one. She was built like a boxcar, sturdy as a freight train, and her hair was dyed an outrageous red.

"Señorita, may I have the pleasure of buying you a drink?"

"Me?" Her voice was like gravel running out the back of a dump truck.

"Yes, you, señorita."

Zapato's instincts were perfect. She was a seaman's widow and lived in the poorer part of the Barrio Chino in Barcelona. She made a scant living in one of the hotels as a maid, and she came to Andora every weekend to buy cheap cigarettes and liquor, which she sold to hotel guests from her cart to make extra money.

At first she glowered when Zapato made it clear that he didn't want to pick her up for the night. But her spirits brightened and her eyes grew interested when he told her what he did want and what she would be paid for it.

"Now, let me understand you, señor," she rasped. "You want me to check into the Hotel Roc and pay in advance for three days?"

"That's right. Then I want you to leave the key in the room and come back to your own hotel here and forget you ever saw me."

She grinned. "That seems like a lot of trouble, señor, just to be with your mistress."

"It is," Zapato said, and shrugged, "but my wife is here in Andorra, and she calls every hotel trying to find us. What can I say?" He took her hand and pressed into it all but a few of his remaining francs. "Will you do it?"

"Why not? Business is business! My name is Jomi Strella."

He waited twenty minutes after she left and then left

himself. Across the street was a large gas station where trucks passing through the tiny country filled up cheaply for the run into Spain. In no time he found a canvas-backed produce truck and climbed under the rear tarp.

No one would see him enter Andorra-la-Vella.

Wearily, Carter opened his eyes. The room was dark. He rolled over, the soft bed giving beneath him.

Strange room.

Then, vaguely, he remembered.

The telephone calls to the countess and Crifasi. The wild, hundred-mile-an-hour ride to the Malaga airport. Meeting Crifasi and his crew in Barcelona, and the caravan up the mountains and into Andorra.

Carter had tried to give orders to help out, but thirty-six hours with only a one-hour nap had gotten to him. Through the countess, they had commandeered a villa in the hills above Andorra-la-Vella, the capital of the little principality, as headquarters for the operation.

When Carter was all but passed out, Crifasi had insisted he hit the sack.

"Feeling better, Nick?"

He turned his head toward the countess's voice. A cigarette glowed from a chair in the center of the room. He sat up.

"Yeah . . . I think."

The cigarette made an upward sweep, glowed bright, and then dimmed. "Want a drag?" she asked.

"Yeah."

He heard her move in the darkness, then her silhouete crossed the window. He felt the bed sink beneath her weight. The cigarette was in front of him. He took it gratefully and put it between his lips. The acrid smoke filtered deep into his lungs.

"When did you get in?"

"A little over six hours ago."

"Christ, what time is it?"

"Almost midnight."

"Damn," Carter hissed, and made to lurch from the bed. Her hands held him.

"There's nothing either of us can do now, Nick. We just have to wait."

Almost gratefully he eased his head back to the pillow. "Are we all set up?"

"It's a good operation," she replied. "Crifasi's people have the rooms next to Lucchi's. When he went out to dinner they got a bug on the phone and in the room. Also, they wired the rental car he picked up in Barcelona. He checked into the room in the name of B. Armandi."

"Czarkis?"

"Nothing yet, but Joe figured he won't come in until tomorrow morning anyway . . . maybe even later. Dolores is in Barcelona trying to get a line on his background."

"What about the thief, Zapato?"

"His name is Felipe Zapato. He's wanted all over Spain, has been for a long time. Your theory is probably right. He must have done a trial run on me at the Seville house, got a look at the network journals, and put two and two together."

Carter nodded. "Then he got a line on Czarkis and made a deal."

She nodded. "Crifasi has also traced the women in that blackmail film."

"And . . .?"

"Sisters . . . Maria and Carla Varga. Maria is dead. And, Nick, she bought it just like Joanna."

"Lucchi."

"Looks that way."

Carter lips drew into a thin line. "When the time comes, he's mine."

The countess put another cigarette between his lips. "Hungry?"

"Yeah, but I don't think I could eat," he sighed.

Her hand came over and the fingers curled through the hair on his chest. "I didn't mean food."

He felt her body move and then slip in beside him. For the first time since he had awakened, he realized that she was naked.

"We're dead in the water until tomorrow," she whispered, a little laugh in her voice.

"What do you suggest in the meantime?"

"Need you ask?"

She pulled him down. Her lips parted, and as she kissed him, he began to feel more relaxed. He began stroking her thighs with the tips of his fingers. He could hardly restrain himself, but he waited. Finally, she moved her hips upward, offering herself to him, and as he moved into her, they found each other's rhythm.

Zapato tapped his fingers against the glass of the booth and waited as the phone rang.

"Hotel Roc."

"Yes, I would like to speak to Señora Jomi Strella, please. I believe she is in four-nineteen."

"No, señor, it is room two-twelve. I will ring her."

"Gracias."

The operator let it ring eight times and came back on the line. "There is no answer, señor."

"Gracias. I will try in the morning."

Zapato hung up, left the booth, and darted into the narrow alley that ran for several blocks between the rolling hills that led up into the mountains and the hotels that lined the main street of Andorra-la-Vella.

Directly behind the Hotel Roc, he easily jumped the low fence to the swimming pool and crossed the courtyard. The rear entrance for the unloading of supplies was of course locked, but his picks made short work of that.

Inside, he moved through the kitchen area and down a narrow, dim corridor to the service stairs used by the maids.

Five minutes later he was inside room 212 and discarding his clothing. He took a long, hot shower, and then slipped between the clean sheets.

This, he thought, looking around at the opulent surroundings, would be the last place anyone would look for him, before or after the switch.

SEVENTEEN

All it took was one rap on the door and the words from Joe Crifasi: "Nick, Tony boy is on the move!" Carter was out of bed, dressed, and downstairs crawling into the car in minutes.

"Where is he headed?"

"Bicisarri," the stocky Italian replied.

Carter nodded. "I know it. There's an old farm road there into Spain, with no frontier post."

"You got it. If he tries to run and hide, Nick, we could be in big trouble. I've only got three people besides myself. And we can't use Bea; she'd be spotted in a minute."

They drove for another twenty minutes in silence, and then, moving around a wide curve, they spotted a cyclist in a cutout ahead.

Crifasi pulled over and leaned from the car. "How are we doing?"

"Mario's got him in the Fiat. He crossed into Spain and went on through Pobla de Segur. He's about halfway to Tremp now."

"Is he still in the Cortina?" Crifasi asked.

"Yes," the cyclist said, nodding. "If you take the N230

171

over the mountain you'll hit him at the Pamplona turn off
. . . if he goes that far."

"Right." The car lurched and both men cursed under their
breaths that they didn't have radios.

Just outside Tremp, Tony Lucchi saw the *Servicio* sign
and pulled in beside the pumps. "Fill it up," he ordered,
and entered the building.

He went immediately to the wall phone and dialed the
number he had found in the envelope that had been left for
him at the desk.

"Yes?"

"It's me."

"Good work, Tony. Now, listen carefully. At eight sharp,
tonight, I will enter the Roc lounge. Zapato might already
be there, or he might come in later. I want you to be at the
bar."

"Yes."

"He will pass me the goods at the table. I will go to the
toilet to inspect. Watch me when I come out. If it is a yes,
I will nod. Use the last booth beside the wall. Do you
understand?"

"Yes, no problem."

"And, Tony, do it very quietly."

"Of course."

"Needless to say, disappear immediately. I suggest you
take a little vacation. In fact, San Sebastian would be nice
this time of the year. You have our contact there?"

"I do."

"He will take care of all our needs. Good-bye, Tony,"

"Ciao."

Tony Lucchi hung up and went back into the sun. He
paid for the gasoline and headed back to Andorra.

Eighteen miles away, near Seo de Urgal on the southern

road out of Andorra, Alexander Czarkis hung up the field phone and nodded at one of the two men across from him.

The man, dressed in white coveralls with a patch on his left breast reading *Teléfono Catalán,* dropped from the rear of the van. He quickly climbed a nearby pole and disconnected two wires, which he carried in a coil back to the white and yellow van that also had the *Teléfono Catalán* logo on its side.

"What now, comrade?" asked the second man in coveralls.

"To Andorra-la-Vella," Czarkis replied. "We will spend the rest of the afternoon laboring studiously behind the Hotel Roc."

At the junction of the N230 and the Pamplona highway, Joe Crifasi turned the car south toward Tremp. Both of them watched anxiously for the Cortina.

Just north of the village, they passed a small service station. The second of Crifasi's men, also on a motorcycle, was waiting beside the road.

"He filled up at that station back there and made a phone call. Then he headed back to Andorra. They have probably picked him up by now, but beyond here, Andorra is the only place he could go."

"Okay," Crifasi said, "get back to the hotel. Maybe we'll pick up something on the bug in Lucchi's room yet."

The man kicked his machine to life and took off. Crifasi pulled back onto the road and headed in the same direction.

"Czarkis is playing it very cagey."

Carter nodded. "We're going to have to nail him right when the trade is made."

"What if he uses a cutout? We'll never know who it is if it isn't Lucchi or if we don't actually see something trade hands."

"Yeah," Carter growled. "Let's just hope little Tony isn't

a decoy and he is in on the trade."

There was one bright light when they got back to the countess's villa. Dolores Martinez had arrived from Barcelona.

She had a complete rundown on Felipe Zapato, including his past record, his detailed description, and a list of everyone in the underworld with whom he had ever done business.

"And that's not all," she said proudly, laying a grainy eight-by-ten photograph on the table in front of Carter. He took one look at it and remembered the outdoor café on the Calle de Sesto in Algeciras.

He had been spotted even with the blind man disguise.

"Czarkis?"

Dolores nodded.

Joe Crifasi entered the room. "You're not gonna believe this."

"Talk to me," Carter said.

"Lucchi is the most cooperative guy I've ever seen. He just made two phone calls. One to the desk for a wake-up call at seven tonight. The other to some guy in San Sebastian. He told the guy that he was coming in by car and to expect him between three and three-thirty in the morning."

Quickly, Carter grabbed a road map of Spain and did some quick calculations. When he was finished, he looked up and smiled.

"Six and a half hours driving time. Whatever it is, it's coming down between seven and nine tonight."

"The question is, where?" Dolores said.

"The hotel," Crifasi replied. "Probably the lounge."

"You're right," Carter said. "The building is like a sieve . . . seven, eight entrances and exits, and the lounge will be jammed with people."

Crifasi reached for the phone. "I'm sure they'll cooperate."

174

"Good," Carter said. "And round us up some hearing-aid walkies and mikes so we can communicate."

The lounge wasn't too large, but it was nearly full by eight o'clock. About the only tables empty were those reserved along the far wall near the exit.

The sliding doors to the kitchen look-through behind the bar were closed except for a one-inch slot. Through that slot, Carter could see practically the entire room.

The hotel staff had been very cooperative. There were six exits. They had agreed to block off two of them. The countess, in a car, was watching both the front exit and the one that went right off the lounge into the street. Dolores, at a flower stall, was watching the side, and one of Crifasi's men was on the lone rear exit still unlocked.

In the lounge itself, the second bartender was Crifasi's, and Joe himself was sitting at the bar.

"Nick . . . ?"

"Go ahead, Bea."

"It's him—your Czarkis character . . . about six feet, three hundred pounds, bullet head, no neck . . ."

"Where?"

"Just going into the hotel."

"Got it. Joe, you read?"

At the bar, Crifasi leaned forward, nodded, and coughed into his tiepin mike.

Through the crack, Carter saw Alexander Czarkis enter the lounge. He exchanged a few words with the hostess, and she escorted him to the table beside the toilets.

"Ramón, where are you?"

"Where else?" came the whisper from behind the bar.

"Where is Lucchi? I can't see him."

"Same stool. I just brought him another drink."

"Check."

Carter nervously smoked a cigarette, then made the rounds

via radio. "Anybody eyeball anybody that looks like Zapato yet?"

All the replies were negative.

Czarkis heaved himself to his feet and lumbered around the corner to the rest rooms.

"Joe . . ."

"I got him. I'll keep an eye on the lobby exit from the john. Let me know when he comes out."

"Roger."

Crifasi slid off his stool and made for the lobby. Ten seconds later he was up on his mike. "Nick, Nick . . ."

"Yeah, Joe, is Czarkis splitting?"

"No, it's him—the thief."

"Zapato?"

"Yeah. The son of a bitch is buying a pack of cigarettes at the kiosk."

"Bea? Dolores?"

"No way, Nick, he didn't come in the front."

"Ditto the side, Nick," Dolores said.

"Not through the rear either, señor. There is a couple making out in a car, and a telephone truck back here. No one has used this door."

"Nick," Crifasi said, "Zapato is coming in."

"And Czarkis is back at his table. Stay in the lobby, Joe. We'll cover in here."

"Check."

Maybe, Carter thought, as Zapato came into the lounge, *the bastard came over the roof.* After all, he figured that would be his usual way of entry. . . .

Felipe Zapato spotted his man at once; he was hard to miss. He brushed his coat with his arm. The false journals were in his inside jacket pocket. The real ones were under his belt at the small of his back.

"Señor, it is good to see you again. I have taken the liberty of ordering wine. Join me."

Zapato nodded and sat down, carefully arranging the long white tablecloth over his lap. Czarkis poured and leaned across the table to speak almost in a whisper.

"I assume, Señor Felipe, that your little run was successful?"

"It was. Where is my money?"

"Where you can get it easily. I will need to examine the merchandise, of course."

"Here?" Czarkis nodded toward the rest rooms. "Sure," Zapato chuckled, "and you go right on out the alley door."

"Foolish, you are foolish," Czarkis said disdainfully. "I will be gone but one minute. With my great bulk, how far ahead of you can I get in one minute, eh?"

Zapato thought for a moment, and then nodded his head in agreement. At the same time, Czarkis felt something drop into his lap. He slipped it inside his coat and turned toward the rest rooms.

"Joe," Carter whispered, "are you still covering the lobby john door?"

"I got it."

"Czarkis is in again. No, wait, he's coming back out again."

"Señor Carter, Ramón here. Lucchi is leaving."

"I've got him," Carter said, peering through the crack. "Joe . . ."

"I got him, Nick. Oh, Christ, what is this, musical piss time? He just went into the john through the lobby door!"

"Excellent, Felipe. Your money is in dollars and pounds, large denominations, two bags."

"Where?"

"The tank of the last booth next to the wall."
Felipe Zapato stood and moved toward the door.

Lucchi stepped through the lobby door and locked it behind him from the inside. He darted to the last stall, moved inside, and climbed up on the toilet and crouched.

From the small of his back he drew his knife and flipped the ugly, curved, eight-inch blade open.

Then he closed the door, took a deep, satisfying breath, and waited.

"Joe, we've got Zapato in the john from this side."
"Lucchi hasn't come out," Crifasi replied. "Should I move in?"
"No, but stay alert. It looks like Lucchi could be the cutout. They're probably making the trade now."

When Zapato pushed the stall door open he had only a fleeting glimpse of the man lunging toward him. Then he felt a powerful punch in his belly and staggered backward.

He hit the row of wash basins and that was when he felt the burning sensation. He looked down and gagged when he saw the hilt of the knife protruding from his belly. Then he saw the hands, grasping the knife and pulling it out of his belly.

When the knife flashed toward him again, Zapato managed to roll to the side. He struck the attendant's chair and grabbed it with both hands.

He stooped and reached for the back of the overturned chair, and hearing the footsteps behind, he swung his body around, bringing the chair up as he did.

It crashed against Lucchi's shoulder, causing him to stumble to one side, and before he could recover fully, the chair was on its return journey, this time aimed at his head.

Lucchi ducked instinctively and Zapato was momentarily thrown off-balance. He recovered quickly enough to swing the chair up again, this time as a shield against Lucchi's oncoming rush. It struck Lucchi's body and Zapato pushed, the knife waving in the air in a vain attempt to reach him. Zapato exerted all his force and kept pushing, moving the other man backward.

Lucchi resisted, hopelessly caught up between the legs of the chair, unable to thrust it aside. He took the only course available: he dropped to the floor, pulling the chair with him but lifting it so it sailed over his head. It still left him at a disadvantage, because he was flat on his back, and he struck out at Zapato's legs with the knife as he lay there.

Zapato drew in his breath as the knife's razor-sharp edge slid along his shinbone, only its angle preventing it from cutting deeply. He tried to leap clear of the thrashing blade as he staggered over Lucchi's sprawled figure and fell heavily against the chair, which had crashed onto the floor just beyond the fallen man's head.

The dapper little killer was starting to come off the floor. Zapato had one chance and he took it. He grasped the chair, shattered it on the counter, and came up with one broken leg in his hand.

Lucchi was lurching up when Zapato drove the spiked chair leg deep into his chest.

Lucchi gasped once and fell to the floor, dead, the knife clattering away.

"Joe, Czarkis just took the alley door from the lounge. Take the two in the john and try to keep it quiet. Bea?"

"I've got him, Nick. He's sauntering down the alley like he hasn't got a care in the world."

"Ramón, take the john from this side. I'll help Mario take Czarkis in the rear."

"Check!"

Carter saw Ramón take off toward the rest room, and he headed toward the rear door of the kitchen.

He wasn't on the earphones to hear Joe Crifasi curse when he found the lobby door locked.

EIGHTEEN

Zapato, using Lucchi's knife, cut three feet from the cloth towel pull and stuffed it under his coat to stop the bleeding.

The bastard, he thought, *the rotten Russian bastard!*

He staggered to the lobby door and found it locked. Through blurred vision he managed to find the twist, then he opened the door and moved into the lobby. He made the stairs and staggered upward. In the mezzanine he saw the open elevator and dived inside.

On the second floor he bounced from wall to wall as he lurched toward room 212.

If he could get in the room, stop the bleeding . . . maybe, just maybe, he would make it.

But, just in case . . .

Through the film that had begun to grow over his eyes, he saw the two mail slots, one for packages, one for letters.

He took the flat, already addressed package from the small of his back and shoved it into the slot. It was barely through when he fell against the wall and slid to the floor.

He crawled, somehow reaching the door to 212. Inside, he bolted and locked the door. Then he tried to get to the window, but the blackness set in and he felt himself falling . . . into darkness.

Carter and Mario rounded the corner side by side, and practically crashed into the countess coming up the alley in the Fiat.

"Did you get him?" she asked.

The two men exchanged quizzical glances.

"You mean he didn't double back to the street?" Carter asked.

"He couldn't," she replied. "I came into the mouth of the alley right away."

"That way!" Carter barked. "I'll take the other side!"

He ran around the rear alley and emerged on the narrow street on the other side. Dolores was still at her flower stand.

"Did he come this way?"

"Hell, no," she cried. "You mean we missed him?"

"Christ," Carter spat, and retraced his steps, only to again meet Mario and the countess.

"Nothing," she said.

"Shit," Carter hissed, pulling the earphones up to his ears from around his neck. "Joe . . ."

"Yeah, here."

"What have you got?"

"A very dead Tony Lucchi."

"Anything on him?" Carter asked.

"Nothing, and there's no Zapato. But, Nick, there's blood all over the place in here. I think Lucchi got in his licks."

"Everybody," Carter barked, "keep the exits covered. Joe, check the roof. Zapato has got to be somewhere in the hotel or going over the roof."

He got affirmatives as he ran toward the front of the hotel.

The traffic was heavy, cars going both ways, trucks making the cut-through from France to Spain, small delivery vans, lots of pedestrians strolling.

But none of them looked remotely like Alexander Czarkis. If he got free of the hotel, it would be like finding a needle in a haystack.

Think, think!

Andorra is a mountain-locked country, no planes, no trains. The only way out is by road or overland, walking. There was no way the overweight Czarkis could walk forty miles over mountains, Carter figured.

Two main roads, through Pas de la Casa on the French side, Seo de Urgel on the Spanish. Both of these had customs checkpoints.

Bicisarri.

It had to be.

"Ramón, Mario . . ."

"Sí?"

"Here, señor."

"Get on the cycles, fast! Get over to the Bicisarri road to Pobla de Segur. That's got to be the way he'll go out. And stay on your radios!"

"Sí."

"Right away."

"Nick, Joe here."

"Yeah, Joe?"

"I found Zapato. Get up to the second floor—fast."

Carter bolted through the lobby. There was confusion everywhere. Hotel staff had sealed off the lounge and the rest rooms. Undoubtedly, they had already called the police.

Ignoring the elevator, Carter ran up the stairs to the second floor. It was pretty easy to see how Crifasi had found Zapato. There was a trail of blood down the hall carpet from the elevator to the door of room 212.

From the looks of it, Zapato had staggered against the steel covering of the mailboxes. Blood was smeared all over them down to the floor.

Crifasi was already taking the room apart when Carter

stepped inside and closed the door behind him.

"Anything?"

"Not yet," Crifasi said. "The body's clean."

For the next twenty minutes, the two men searched the room, but they found nothing.

"Señor . . . Ramón here."

"Go ahead, Ramón."

"We are at the Bicisarri crossing. So far three cars and a tractor. Nothing. The cars were all Minis. That whale could never fit in the trunk of one of those."

"Stay with it," Carter barked, and he and Crifasi resumed their search.

Twenty minutes later, they gave up and slumped into chairs.

"It's no use," Crifasi said. "He must have passed them over to Czarkis."

Carter nodded. "Let's get out of here before we have more explaining to do than we can handle."

The two men picked up Dolores and walked the short distance to where Beatriz sat in the Fiat. While Crifasi clued them in, Carter got back on the walkies.

"Ramón, how are we doing?"

"Two more cars, negative, and a produce van. We stopped the van as though we wanted to buy some vegetables. Nothing there, either."

Carter sighed. "And that's it?"

"That's it, Señor Nick. Oh, and a telephone van is parked at the crossroads. One man is up a pole working on the lines."

"Okay," Carter said, "we're coming your way."

"Sí."

"Move over," Carter said, "I'll drive."

The countess slid over in the seat and Carter took the wheel.

Two blocks down the main street, it hit him.

"Ramón . . . Ramón!"

"Right here."

"Is Mario there?"

"*Sí*, I am here."

"Mario, you said earlier that there was a couple in a car and a telephone van behind the hotel. Is it the same van that is working out there now?"

"*Sí*, I recognize the man on the pole."

Carter floored the Fiat.

They were set. Mario and Ramón were in the rocks above the truck on both sides. Crifasi was coming from the front. Carter had inched up the road, going from rock to rock until he was less than thirty yards from the rear of the van.

The countess and Dolores had driven past the van and just around the curve a hundred yards in front of it. There, they would park the Fiat sideways across the road.

They didn't have much time. Carter had already guessed what Alexander Czarkis was doing. The line from the truck up to the telephone lines on the pole was a cut-in. Evidently, Czarkis wasn't taking any chances. He wasn't waiting until Madrid to make the pass. He was phoning in the contacts of the network to someone from here.

"Bea . . . ?"

"Yes, we're set, Nick."

"Okay, everybody, here we go." Carter moved up another ten yards, leveled the Luger over a boulder, and shouted, "Czarkis, it's Carter. You've got three seconds."

All hell broke loose.

The rear of the van flew open and a man in white coveralls began spraying with a machine pistol. Carter returned the fire and got two hits. The man screamed and hit the deck.

The one on the pole tried to come down. Mario nailed him with a whole magazine and he hung, dead, on his safety belt.

In the meantime, Crifasi opened up from the front and

Ramón from the side. It sounded like World War III as bullets tore out glass and ricocheted off steel.

Over it all, Carter heard the roar of the engine and the van started moving.

"Joe, he's coming your way!"

"I got him."

Carter ran as hard as he could, but the rear of the van slipped through his fingers. He fell on his belly, and through the rear window saw the fat man fight the wheel to swerve around Crifasi's withering fire.

"Nick, I think I winged him!"

"Yeah," Carter grunted, on his feet and running, "but he's still moving."

Together, they ran like hell. Just short of the curve, they heard the grinding sound of metal against rock and a crash.

They rounded the curve and took it all in with one look.

Czarkis had spotted the Fiat and had tried to climb a bank to get around it. He had gotten around the Fiat, but he had been unable to right the truck.

Now it was on its side, and Czarkis was staggering from the rear doors, a machine pistol in his right hand, the leather-bound books in his left.

Carter and Crifasi went to their knees.

"You're through, Czarkis!" the Killmaster barked.

The machine pistol swung around and both agents opened fire. The huge body absorbed slugs like toothpicks in jelly.

But they took their toll. Czarkis staggered, blood gushing from a half-dozen holes in his big body.

Crifasi ended it with a head shot that tore away half the man's face.

Carter ran forward and yanked the books from the dead man's hand.

"Everyone, in the Fiat! Ramón, Mario—use your cycles! Let's get out of here before the Guardia arrives!"

The women were already in the car. Carter threw the two books on the countess's lap and swerved the Fiat around.

A hundred yards down the road, the countess cried, "Nick . . ."

"What?"

"They're phonys!"

"What?"

"The books. This isn't my handwriting. And we don't have to worry about Czarkis relaying names. All of these names are phony!"

Carter slammed the steering wheel. "Zapato. It had to be Zapato!"

It was four in the morning and the street was empty. The three of them sat in the Fiat, smoking in silence.

"Here she comes," Dolores Martinez said.

Beatriz covered the last few yards to the car and slipped into the rear seat.

"Your guess was right, Nick. They've cleaned up the wall and the front of the mailboxes, but when I shined the light down the mail chute, I saw it . . . blood."

"Okay, wait here," Carter murmured.

"What are you going to do?" Crifasi asked.

"Zapato was a good thief. Let's see if I can come close."

Getting into the hotel was a cinch. Cracking the tiny mailroom behind the larger room containing the safe-deposit boxes would be a little harder.

Carter had stayed many times at the Hotel Roc in years past, and he remembered that in certain rooms he had been awakened in the night by street noises.

All of the hotel doors fastened with a spring lock and a strong inner bolt, and Carter was too cautious to attempt a break-in from a brightly lit hotel corridor in any event. He needed darkness in which to operate. He discovered a tiny light well that offered a safe, hidden passage down through the interior of the building.

He chose a room on the third-floor rear. He knocked first. When he got no response, he picked the lock and entered.

He breathed a sigh of relief when his memory proved accurate. The bathroom window opened onto a light well. It was a narrow, rectangular shaft falling from a skylight on the roof to the basement level. Two small windows, paned with frosted glass for the sake of guests' privacy, faced each other in opposite walls at each floor.

The forward wall from the windows housed the mail chute. Carter guessed that somewhere near the bottom there would be a latch that could be opened in case something was clogging the chute.

He removed the window, stripped to his shorts, and went down the light well with a screwdriver in his teeth. He did it like a mountain climber works clefts in the rocks, back and feet braced against the blank walls.

Just below the mezzanine floor, he found the hatch. Eight screws released, and he eased through the opening.

His second guess also proved correct. The chute was about three feet thick here, to take the larger packages from the shops and offices on the mezzanine floor.

He took a deep breath, let go, and sailed down the chute. He came out in a tiny, one-doored room, lit with a yellow bulb, and landed in an overflowing basket of mail.

It took him nearly an hour of digging, but he finally spotted it: brown, blood-stained wrapping, addressed to Alberto Ferare, 24 Calle Sierra, Madrid, Spain.

To make sure, he slit the paper and removed the books. Page by page he flipped through them until he found the name that would prove it all: Joanna Dubshek.

There was no doubt that these were the originals. There was also no doubt that the thief had bargained away Joanna's life.

SPYKILLER

The Killmaster knee-walked his way back up through the building, replacing the vents and hatch covers along the way. Back in the room, he dressed.

In the hall, he started to exit the hotel, as he had entered, with stealth.

But suddenly he was tired of stealth. There had been enough of it the last few days. He entered the elevator and poked the lobby button.

The concierge, a young man with dark, boyish good looks, flashed him a smile and opened one of the glass lobby doors. The morning was bright and already warm.

"Buenos dias, señor. It looks like a lovely day."

"Yes," Carter replied, "a very lovely day indeed."

He hit the sidewalk and turned toward the car, carrying the two leather-bound books in his swinging right hand.

Even at that distance, through the windshield he could see the tears of relief well up in the countess's eyes.

DON'T MISS THE NEXT NEW
NICK CARTER SPY THRILLER
BOLIVIAN HEAT

"He is late," said one of the men.

"No longer, *amigo*," Prida replied. "Look to the door."

Carter entered, still carrying the briefcase. He stood by the door, surveying the room's occupants. Prida and company were not hard to spot.

"*Buenos tardes*," he said at last. "Señor Prida?"

"*Sí*. Welcome to Las Polpas, señor, the armpit of the Sierra Madres. Sit. Luis, tequila."

After introductions were made, the men moved to a table in a dark corner of the room. The bartender brought a bottle of tequila and placed it in the middle of the table along with a tray of narrow glases, wedges of lime, and a shaker of salt.

Carter had been in many meets like this. There would be small talk, then fringe talk, then big talk. During all of it they would drink. By the time a deal was struck, the bottle would be "down to the worm." If the deal was acceptable, the two agreeing parties would eat the worm.

A speaker across the room blared mariachi music. Patrons

at the bar and the other tables drank, conversed, ate the snacks the bartender's wife occasionally brought from the kitchen, and all the while kept their attention curiously half-directed at Prida and the *norteamericano* at his table.

The bandit chief lifted his glass. With a broad smile that bared his amazingly white teeth amid the darkly tangled rubble of his beard, he toasted his guest. The crossed bandoliers on his chest rubbed against each other, and their strings of bullets had the kind of effect he intended when he wore them.

"*Salud,*" he said.

The others lifted their glasses to him and drank.

It took only two shots around to get the small talk out of the way. When Prida poured again, the altered expression on his face told Carter what was coming next.

"We will talk of money, business, and how we may enjoy the evening, in that order," he said. "You have the money, *amigo?*"

"Yes," Carter replied. "Here in this briefcase. Do you want to go somewhere so you can check it out?"

"Lay it on the table, *amigo*. We will examine it here."

Carter looked around the room, then lifted the briefcase from the floor. He laid it flat and pushed it toward Prida.

The man rested his arms on it and clasped his hands. He laughed again. "Do not be alarmed, my gringo friend," he said. "I want all to see it. I want them to see with their own eyes the wealth Prida brings to Las Polpas."

"The town knows about what we're doing?" Carter asked incredulously.

"No, no, no, my friend. I want them to know only that Prida brings wealth, not how he brings it. The mystery loses its value when it is no longer a mystery."

He flipped the catches on the briefcase and opened it. Stacks of American currency filled it snugly.

Prida smiled broadly, and when he was sure everyone in

the cantina had seen the contents of the briefcase, he dropped the lid.

"You are a man of honor, *amigo*. Now, what do you require of me and my people?"

"In a few days, perhaps a week, there will be a cocaine run from the south up to Mexico City. I want to hijack the product."

Prida pushed the briefcase back across the table to Carter. "Señor, I do many things. I am a bad *hombre*. I have killed many times, but only with honor. This dope business hurts many people. I want nothing—"

"Señor Prida," Carter interrupted, "let me finish."

He went on with the last of the plan, the final resting place of the dope, the transportation of Prida and his men in and out of Bolivia. By the time he had finished, there were no smiles but the frowns had disappeared.

"Excuse us, señor."

The three men rose and moved to the front of the cantina. They talked for several minutes in low tones with vigorous gestures and what appeared to be anger. When they returned, the two lieutenants sat, Prida paced.

"I can put twenty men on the job, señor. How many will we be facing on the hijack?"

Carter shrugged. "I don't know that yet."

"And this raid on the refinery in Bolivia . . . how many there?"

"I don't know that, either," Carter replied.

Prida sighed. "Señor, you make a decision very difficult, even in exchange for the great amount of money you offer."

"We will have surprise, complete surprise, on our side. And more than enough arms to do the job."

"Perhaps," the other man said, scratching his ratty beard, "but my men do not trust you, a man who does not have all the facts."

Carter lit a cigarette and slowly shifted his gaze around

the table. "And what would convince them to trust me?"

It was Prida's turn to shrug. "Perhaps they would follow you if they knew of your courage, señor."

"I have the courage to face both of them with my hands and them with knives."

Prida chuckled. "No, señor, that would be foolish for both of us. I can see in your eyes . . . I would lose two good men. Can you stand pain?"

The other men looked at Carter with expectant faces. The men at the bar began gravitating toward the table.

"As much as any other man," Carter replied.

The bandit leader leaned forward and pulled a knife from a sheath at his belt. In the same motion he drove the point into the table. It quivered, the steel blue, the edge like a razor.

"It's sharp. Feel it!"

"I can see that it's sharp."

"Luis!"

The bartender came over, smiling broadly. He grasped the knife and yanked it from the table. Prida laid his right arm out, the palm up, and held it with his left.

"Ready?" the bartender said.

"Sí, amigo," Prida replied. "Have the good eye."

The knife struck cleanly into Prida's palm and through to the table underneath. His fingers curled up reflexively, then he straightened them. The hand was pinned motionless to the table.

He looked up at Carter, his eyes gleaming. "See?"

"I see."

"Take it out, Luís, be quick."

The knife was yanked out in one quick jerk and the wound doused with tequila.

"Well, señor, what do you say?"

Calmly, Carter dropped his cigarette on the floor and

ground it out beneath his heel. "One thing. Luís?"

"*Sí?*"

"Clean the knife."

Carter positioned his arm on the table much the same as Prida had done, the fingers splayed, the vein at the wrist rising blue under the skin.

"The knife is clean. Señor?"

"Ready," Carter said.

The knife struck with incredible force, pinning his hand to the table. There was no pain at first, only the shock of impact. He moved his fingers and the pain came, sharp, darting up to his elbow.

"Good," Prida said. "Luís?"

The knife was removed and Carter looked around the table and up at Prida. "Well?"

The bandit leader nodded and reached for the bottle of tequila.

"Now, señor, we will eat the worm."

—From BOLIVIAN HEAT
A New Nick Carter Spy Thriller
From Jove in July 1988

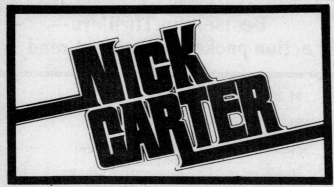

☐ 0-441-14222-2	**DEATH HAND PLAY**	$2.50
☐ 0-515-09055-7	**EAST OF HELL**	$2.75
☐ 0-441-21877-6	**THE EXECUTION EXCHANGE**	$2.50
☐ 0-441-45520-4	**THE KREMLIN KILL**	$2.50
☐ 0-441-24089-5	**LAST FLIGHT TO MOSCOW**	$2.50
☐ 0-441-51353-0	**THE MACAO MASSACRE**	$2.50
☐ 0-441-57502-1	**NIGHT OF THE WARHEADS**	$2.50
☐ 0-441-58612-0	**THE NORMANDY CODE**	$2.50
☐ 0-441-57283-9	**TUNNEL FOR TRAITORS**	$2.50
☐ 0-515-09112-X	**KILLING GAMES**	$2.75
☐ 0-515-09214-2	**TERMS OF VENGEANCE**	$2.75
☐ 0-515-09168-5	**PRESSURE POINT**	$2.75
☐ 0-515-09255-X	**NIGHT OF THE CONDOR**	$2.75
☐ 0-515-09324-6	**THE POSEIDON TARGET**	$2.75
☐ 0-515-09376-9	**THE ANDROPOV FILE**	$2.75
☐ 0-515-09444-7	**DRAGONFIRE**	$2.75
☐ 0-515-09490-0	**BLOODTRAIL TO MECCA**	$2.75
☐ 0-515-09519-2	**DEATHSTRIKE**	$2.75
☐ 0-441-74965-8	**SAN JUAN INFERNO**	$2.50
☐ 0-441-57280-4	**THE KILLING GROUND**	$2.50
☐ 0-515-09547-8	**LETHAL PREY**	$2.75
☐ 0-515-09584-2	**SPYKILLER** (on sale June '88)	$2.95
☐ 0-515-09646-6	**BOLIVIAN HEAT** (on sale July '88)	$2.95
☐ 0-515-09681-4	**THE RANGOON MAN** (on sale August '88)	$2.95
☐ 0-515-09706-3	**CODE NAME COBRA** (on sale September '88)	$2.95

Please send the titles I've checked above. Mail orders to:

BERKLEY PUBLISHING GROUP
390 Murray Hill Pkwy., Dept. B
East Rutherford, NJ 07073

NAME _____

ADDRESS _____

CITY _____

STATE _____ ZIP _____

Please allow 6 weeks for delivery.
Prices are subject to change without notice.

POSTAGE & HANDLING:
$1.00 for one book, $.25 for each
additional. Do not exceed $3.50.

BOOK TOTAL	$_____
SHIPPING & HANDLING	$_____
APPLICABLE SALES TAX (CA, NJ, NY, PA)	$_____
TOTAL AMOUNT DUE	$_____
PAYABLE IN US FUNDS. (No cash orders accepted.)	

Bestselling Thrillers —
action-packed for a great read